angels like me

Karen McCombie

PUFFIN

PUFFIN BOOKS

UK | USA | Canada | Ireland | Australia
India | New Zealand | South Africa

Puffin Books is part of the Penguin Random House group of companies
whose addresses can be found at global.penguinrandomhouse.com.

puffinbooks.com

First published 2015
002

Set in 13/20pt Baskerville MT Std
Typeset by Jouve (UK), Milton Keynes
Printed and bound in Great Britain by Clays Ltd, Elcograf S.p.A.

A CIP catalogue record for this book is available from the British Library

ISBN: 978-0-141-34456-0

www.greenpenguin.co.uk

MIX
Paper from
responsible sources
FSC® C018179

Penguin Random House is committed to a
sustainable future for our business, our readers
and our planet. This book is made from Forest
Stewardship Council® certified paper.

*For Damie Joyce, who's a little ray of sunshine,
with hair the colour of sunsets*

Contents

I wish I could tell . . .

I have something amazing to say.

And I want to YELL it from the top of this hill.

But shy girls like me aren't so good at yelling, so I do something else.

'Happy New Year, Riley Roberts,' I whisper instead.

Here's what's amazing – I hadn't expected to be happy this year.

But then I hadn't expected my new next-door neighbours to end up being my best friends.

Or that they'd be real-life angels . . .

'Oi, Riley!'

That's my *other* new best friend, calling out to me as he goofs around, waving at me to join in. Woody's not an angel, in case you were wondering. He's more of a dork, but that's OK. In fact, it's a lot of fun.

'In a second,' I call out to him, resting my back against a large block of white marble.

Perched on the block is another angel, wings and all. But this one's made of stone, a statue who's been staring out from the top of Folly Hill for a couple of hundred years or more.

Copying her, I take in the view too, but use my camera to pan around and film the jumble of streets and buildings of the town. Dad's print shop is down there on the High Road; the hospital where his girlfriend, Hazel, works is that big white block; and down by the station, that's where Mum's florist's was, though that's long gone now . . .

'Aw, c'mon, Riley!' begs Woody, as he rushes by, chasing my little sort-of-stepsister, Dot. 'Put down the camera and help me catch her!'

'In a sec!' I say again, smiling at the two of them as they lollop around like a pair of puppies.

The thing is, I'm not in the mood to play some dumb, but fun, game *quite* yet.

Just for a minute, I want to hold on to my happy new-year feeling. I'm just *so* glad to be back here after two weeks away. The whole of the Christmas holidays was spent in relatives' overheated houses or stuck in our stuffy car on endless motorways between visits.

All that time – even when I was having fun, getting nice presents, staying up late on New Year's Eve – I kept pining for home. Well, for Sunshine, Kitt and Pearl, really . . .

Before I went away, when we were saying our byes and see-you-soons, Pearl had hugged me and said, 'Oh, I can't WAIT till you're back, Riley. It's going to be amazing!'

I'd been about to ask her what she meant, but then Dad had honked the car horn for me to hurry up and there was no time. Apart from that, Sunshine

and Kitt looked wary, the way they do when they think Pearl has said too much . . .

So I won't make a big deal of it when I see them. I won't ask and risk getting Pearl into trouble. I'll just be patient and see what unfolds.

Maybe the girls are going to tell me more about themselves. (I know their present, but not much about their past or future.)

Or maybe they'll let me help find the next person who needs fixing. (I don't have nine angelic skills like *they* do, but I'll do my best.)

Or perhaps they'll keep their promise and find out more about Mum for me (since Dad won't tell me *anything*).

Thinking of my special friends, I feel a flutter of nervous excitement in my tummy and lower my camera, glancing towards the semicircles of roads at the foot of the hill.

One of them is Chestnut Crescent. It's easy to make out because of the giant, solid chestnut tree in the garden of number thirty-three, the house

next door to mine. My best friend Tia used to live there, but she's far away on the other side of the world, probably plunging into a pool in the New Zealand summer.

Here, of course, it's winter, and number thirty-three is now home to my new, *magical* best friends.

I just hope they hurry up and come – the air up here is so frost-prickly cold that my bare fingers are in danger of falling off. (Yes, Hazel was annoyingly right when she shouted after me that I'd need my gloves today.)

'Arf! Arf! Arf!'

I jump as a small log is shoved in front of my face.

It has two googly eyes stuck on it, and a nose and mouth drawn on long ago (by me) in marker pen. It's Dot's beloved pet 'dog', Alastair: a lumpy, bumpy chunk of driftwood that does look vaguely like a pooch if you squint at it funny.

It doesn't bark for real, though. My dorky friend Woody is helping out with the sound effects.

'Fancy translating?' I ask him. Woody grins at me, his gelled spikes of dark hair flopping forward on to his forehead.

'*I* will!' Dot bursts in first, full of bouncy five-year-old enthusiasm. 'Alastair wants you to come and play, Riley. NOW!'

She grabs my stiff, cold fingers in her fuzzy, warm mittens, but I resist. 'I'm fine here, looking at the view,' I tell her.

'*What* view?' Dot frowns, coming to stand next to me. 'It's just buildings and cars and BORING stuff.'

OK, so views are about as exciting as a trip to the paint aisle of a DIY store when you're a kid.

'It's not *all* boring!' I say, wondering how I can make it interesting for her. 'Why don't you try to imagine what the Angel statue saw when she was first here, years and years ago?'

My little sort-of-stepsister looks up at me, then gazes thoughtfully around.

'Did she see dinosaurs?' Dot finally suggests.

I laugh. 'She's not *that* old!'

I'm just about to tell Dot that, back in the early 1800s, the Angel would've looked out on:

- fields upon fields of crops and cows (instead of rows upon rows of streets and houses)
- the grand Hillcrest Manor (though my modern, blocky secondary school has taken its place)
- a winding country track called Meadow Lane (now a noisy dual carriageway, still – stupidly – called Meadow Lane)
- an ornamental lake named after the daughter of some posh old lord of Hillcrest (which is a scruffy, bramble-tangled dog-walkers' spot these days).

But, before I can speak, Dot's mind – as usual – jumps off like a frog.

'What's your New Year Wish, Riley?' she turns and asks me.

7

'My New Year Wish?' I check with her. 'Don't you mean my new year's *resolution*?'

Dot narrows her eyes, as if I've just spoken to her in an ancient Inca dialect. 'No. Not one of *them*,' she says with an earnest shake of the head. 'Your New Year *Wish*.'

I turn my snigger into a thoughtful '*Hmm . . .*' and do some fake-thinking. Meanwhile, Dot slips off her mittens and flaps her hands madly.

'*My* New Year Wish is that I could be a penguin and fly to the Arctic!' she trills, and spins.

Woody and me, we swap quick glances. Of course, one of us *could* be a spoilsport and point out that penguins actually:

a) live in the *Ant*arctic and
b) don't fly.

Luckily for Dot, neither of us are that mean. And, hey, she'll learn stuff like that in class soon enough. Maybe even tomorrow, since it's the first day of term.

'Wow, that sounds great, Dot!' Woody says instead. 'Well, for *my* New Year Wish, I'd like to bring an extinct dodo back to life, and it could fly with you!'

'Yay!' cheers Dot, too busy flapping to spot Woody winking at me.

Wait a minute – what's that smudged all over Dot's nails? Pale blue varnish with sparkles in it. Exactly like the nail varnish Sunshine, Kitt and Pearl bought me as a Christmas present. In fact, it *is* the nail varnish that Sunshine, Kitt and Pearl bought me as a Christmas present.

I'm just about to give Dot a slightly stern big sort-of-stepsister talk about using things without asking permission when I see them . . .

(My heart thud-thuds.)

Three girls – and their white-blond fuzzy dog – meandering up the crunchy flint path that leads here, to the Angel, and to us.

Sunshine is the tallest, her waist-length wavy hair fluttering around her head like a rust-red festival banner.

Beside her, shorter, is Kitt, the lenses of her thick black-rimmed glasses catching the light.

Pearl waves at me, and, even though she's too far away for me to see her face clearly, I know she'll be smiling, because she's the cutest, friendliest person I've ever met. Even if she isn't *technically* a person . . .

I wave back, and know instantly what my REAL New Year Wish would be: I wish I could tell the world that these girls are angels.

Actual, amazing, awesome angels.

And I wish I could tell the world something else, something I can hardly believe: that these amazing, awesome angels *like* me. Ordinary, mortal, un-amazing ME!

Dot spots that I'm not paying her any attention and looks where *I'm* looking. As soon as she sees Sunshine, Kitt and Pearl, she takes off, shrieking 'HELLOOOOO!' as she hurtles down the hill, all ready to give their dog, Bee, a hug.

Then I notice Dot slow down. I think she's confused and it's obvious why. Instead of waving

back, the three girls have turned away from her and are staring around in different directions, as if the view is calling to them.

Which it is, sort of.

'What are they doing?' Woody asks, frowning at our friends. Of course, he doesn't know what *I* know.

He doesn't know what Sunshine, Kitt and Pearl really are.

He doesn't know they're trainee angels, or that they have hidden-away wings that could unfurl before his very eyes.

He doesn't know they're learning how to use their skills to heal troubled hearts.

He doesn't know *I* was the very first person who they helped.

He doesn't know he was the second.

He doesn't know that right at this moment Sunshine, Kitt and Pearl are 'seeking', trying to tune into the THIRD person who's lost their shine.

He doesn't know that today, tomorrow or very

soon a new adventure will begin for someone, thanks to those three strange girls.

But what *I* don't realize is that I've been grinning to myself while I've been thinking about all of this.

'You know something?' says Woody, waggling Alastair the log dog in my face. 'I think you're as weird as they are, Riley Roberts.'

Ha! If only he knew the truth . . .

Three shades of blue

The shimmer of a peacock feather. (Sunshine.)

Any shade the sky happens to be. (Kitt.)

Piercing pale husky. (Pearl.)

Gaze into each of the angels' eyes and their intense colour will give you the shivers.

My eyes? If you want to know, they're muddy-puddle brown (boo).

It's not only a question of eye colour. The truth is, in every way, I could never be as weird and wonderful as Sunshine, Kitt and Pearl. I'll never have their talents, their wings, their effortless cool at school. And I'll never have what Pearl once showed me: a silk bag full of shimmering, trembling 'marbles' – tiny orbs that glow brighter the more her skills grow.

So, yeah, I'm hopelessly ordinary Riley Roberts, but I'll happily settle for being the angels' friend, for peeking into their world whenever they let me.

And here and now, sitting in assembly, they're letting me . . .

'I want you all to think of today, this new term, as a fresh start,' Mr Thomlinson, our deputy headteacher, is saying up on the stage. 'I want to see positive attitudes to your work. I want to see . . .'

As Mr Thomlinson talks, Pearl leans her elbow on my shoulder, and instantly I feel a low, intense vibration. (It makes the hairs on my arms prickle and tickle.)

I know what it is, of course. All three girls are concentrating hard, using one of their nine skills to scan the school hall, hoping to find the next person

who needs their help, the next person who's lost their shine.

But the vibration is as far as it goes for me; I don't sense the world the way the angels do. So while my friends quietly tune in, scanning and seeking, all I'm aware of is Mr Thomlinson droning on about his expectations of us.

Though I'm also aware of the students around me, I guess.

Everyone's either:

- listening politely,
- *pretending* to listen politely but daydreaming about something else, or
- ignoring Mr Thomlinson altogether and chatting to their mates.

When it comes to that last point, I'm talking about queen of mean Lauren Mayhew and her two horrible best buddies, Joelle and Nancy.

Unfortunately, they're in my form class, and are currently sitting in the row in front of me.

'And now on to something rather exciting,' booms Mr Thomlinson.

'I bet it's not!' hisses Lauren, tossing her long blonde hair over the back of her chair, practically letting it land on my lap. Joelle and Nancy sit either side of her, snickering like a pair of pet hyenas.

'Some of you,' Mr Thomlinson continues, 'may well have seen posters around town publicizing the Frost Fair that's happening next Saturday.'

'Told you!' says Lauren, yawning theatrically. Next thing, she stuffs some chewing gum in her mouth and starts chomp-chomp-chomping loudly.

I glance down the end of the row at our form teacher, Mrs Mahoney, who hasn't noticed what Lauren's up to.

'For those who don't know, the last Frost Fair happened here during the very cold winter of 1814. It was held on the frozen ice of Lady Grace's Lake,

when the lake itself was part of the extensive Hillcrest estate.'

Lauren yawns louder.

Joelle and Nancy are giddy with sniggers.

Still Mrs Mahoney doesn't seem to notice.

It's so unfair! Anyone else would get the glower of gloom for being disruptive (even *I* have), but Lauren's just one of those teacher-friendly girls who miraculously gets away with it.

'Needless to say, the present-day Frost Fair isn't going to be on ice. First, because there's no ice, and, second, it would, of course, be banned for health and safety reasons!' Mr Thomlinson tries to joke. No one laughs. 'But it will be held *around* the lake, as a fundraiser. Organizers are hoping to get enough money to restore the site to its former glory.'

'Wow, I couldn't be *less* interested,' whispers Lauren, tossing her head back again; finding her own sneering words incredibly funny, I'm sure.

Wow, she is SO rude, I think to myself, moving to

avoid her stupid glossy hair, which is now actually brushing my knees.

'And what's exciting is that our school has been invited to send students to perform at the fair.'

'Yesss! *Now* you're talking. Me and my girls will have a bit of that,' says Lauren, while Joelle and Nancy join in with air punches and act like Lauren's the most entertaining – and not the most annoying – person in the history of Hillcrest Academy. 'Bring it on! We're the best!'

I gaze over at Mrs Mahoney, but she's still missing this. Then I notice that I'm being stared at by Sunshine, Kitt and Pearl.

'You're a little bit purple, Riley,' Pearl whispers, her blonde eyebrows all furrowed with worry.

Uh-oh. Stress shows up as a mauve cloud, Pearl once told me. Through the angels' eyes I must have a halo of it hovering over me now, which means my friends can sense I'm wound up, but they don't know why.

I can hardly say it out loud, of course. But there

is a way I can tell them what I'm thinking, without being caught by Mrs Mahoney . . . I can let the girls read my mind. All I have to do is relax and let them in.

So – deep, slow breath – that's what I do.

Three sets of differently blue eyes momentarily darken to something stormier.

They read me, I'm sure.

Then, surprisingly, all three turn their gaze back to the front of the hall and carry on listening – or pretending to listen – to what Mr Thomlinson has to say.

Huh? Is that *it*? They really aren't at *all* interested in my feelings?

I guess maybe Sunshine, Kitt and Pearl think my irritation with Lauren is silly and unimportant. (They think LOTS of human emotions are silly and unimportant.)

But then Lauren *did* bully me when my old friend Tia moved away, so you can't exactly blame me for being her biggest non-fan . . .

'So if anyone's keen to represent the school at this important local event,' Mr Thomlinson carries on, 'then please come to the auditions being held here in the hall tomorrow lunchtime.'

'*We'll* be there, so no point any losers bothering to show up, right?' I hear Lauren say boastfully to her friends, before she bends over and grabs her bag, ready to leave the millisecond Mr Thomlinson says we're excused.

'All right, you may all leave . . .'

The rest of our deputy head's sentence – 'calmly and quietly' – is lost in the general shuffle and screech of chairs.

It's only when I'm trundling along the line behind Sunshine, Kitt and Pearl that I hear *another* kind of screech – a girl kind.

'Eurgh! I've got *chewing* gum stuck in my hair! How did THAT happen?'

I don't turn round.

There's no *way* I want Lauren to see my pleased smirk and think *I* had anything to do with her current hair disaster. But I reckon I know who *did* have something to do with it . . .

'Pearl?' I whisper, crushing up behind her as we inch towards the end of the row of chairs.

She used errant magic just now, didn't she?

She isn't supposed to.

First, because the angels are only ever meant to use their magic for positive, good, important reasons, not for petty tit-for-tat human reasons.

And, second, because the angels need all their energy to develop the nine skills, and using magic for anything else just sucks that energy away. It's like leaving a torch on and letting the light fade to nothing as the batteries run down.

But still, Pearl's messed up and messed around with errant magic before. The chart on the wall of the girls' loft bedroom – the one that lists their progress with the skills – has a bundle of black crosses against her name because of it.

'What?' says Pearl, glancing over her shoulder at me.

Her eyes are their normal colour: the pale grey-blue of a husky dog's. They're not darkening, or twinkling, and her mouth isn't crinkling into a don't-tell secret smile.

OK, so it doesn't look like Pearl's guilty of letting her feelings get the better of her. *This* time . . .

'Um, nothing, doesn't matter,' I say quickly.

Well, if *Pearl* didn't do the magic . . . was it Kitt? Kitt is so serious, and works hard at getting her skills right. But buried deep is a temper. And during last term's school trip to the theme park a flash of Kitt's anger turned Lauren into a shrieking, shaking, spider-covered mess on the Haunted House ride. (Lauren deserved it, trust me.)

I peek past Pearl at Kitt, just to check for any signs of revenge rage on my behalf. But all I see is Kitt pushing her glasses up on to her nose, her expression still and earnest.

So if it wasn't Pearl and Kitt . . . but it *couldn't* have been Sunshine. She is dreamy, calm and pretty much perfect. Sunshine never, *ever* breaks the rules –

unless it's to sort out the mess her sisters have got themselves into.

I hear Lauren shriek some more. 'DO something, Joelle! Get it out NOW! Ouch! You're *hurting* me!'

Hey, I think, smiling to myself, *maybe I should just think of Lauren's bad luck as a small, surprise present to me.*

And worry about *who* did the magic later . . .

Watch the wonder

People stare.

They always do.

This lunchtime, like every lunchtime, Sunshine, Kitt and Pearl stroll along the corridor and heads turn. Girls and boys in every year group are drawn like magnets to these strangely cool girls.

Sunshine, Kitt and Pearl, meanwhile, have absolutely *no* idea that they're strange, or cool, or even that anyone's staring.

Sunshine has never noticed that girls are copying her habit of wearing her ankle boots unlaced and of clipping her long hair up on one side with a flutter of coloured butterfly clips.

Kitt is oblivious to the fact that heaps more students are wearing black geek glasses now, or that twisting your hair into a cute pair of buns has become a big fashion.

Pearl hums happily to herself, not spotting the stubby plaits she's inspired or the stripy socks and tights that everyone's wearing – unless they're a boy, of course. (Or Lauren Mayhew and her cronies, who stick to their personal uniform of long, flicky hair, rolled-up micro skirts and sneers.)

You know, it's a lot of fun to stroll alongside the girls and watch the wonder in everyone's faces.

And I bet plenty of people wonder why Sunshine, Kitt and Pearl let little old me hang out with them.

'You wouldn't understand,' I feel like telling them all. 'They're *angels*. They take the time to know me and they *like* me!'

But, same as yesterday – when I was dreaming up a New Year 'Wish' for Dot – I keep quiet.

'Hi!' says Woody, bounding towards us and interrupting my thoughts.

'Hi,' I reply, and I'm the only one of us who stops to talk.

Sunshine, Kitt and Pearl say nothing, since they're lost in their senses: searching, seeking. They breeze past Woody, as if he's as noticeable as a twirling speck of dust – and not a tall, skinny, freckle-nosed twelve-year-old.

'Was it something I said?' he asks me jokily, while Sunshine, Kitt and Pearl disappear into the bustle of blazers on the move. I'd like to go after them, of course, to see if I can help them in some way, but I can hardly ignore Woody, can I?

And I can't exactly tell him the truth: *Yeah, they're just busy seeking at the moment. Do you want to know what that is? And what the rest of their skills are?*

I wrote a note once, trying to remind myself what every skill was and what it meant. I threw it away

(of course), since it was for my eyes only. But could you imagine if I had it in my pocket right now and I let Woody see it?

THE NINE SKILLS:

- *SEEKING: tuning into someone's thoughts or feelings*
- *QUIET WORDS: talking with no sound*
- *VIRTUAL STROKING: infusing someone with a sense of happiness (starting with a touch, but doing it from afar)*
- *WARMTH: stopping a person panicking with a feeling of cascading warm water spilling over them*
- *SPRINGING: making someone tell you what's on their mind, without them meaning to (like a truth drug)*
- *CATCHING: seeing JUST into the future – phones about to ring, people coming round a corner, etc.*
- *SPIRIT LIFTING: cheering someone up by letting them relive – just for a few seconds – a treasured memory*
- *TELLING (the second strongest skill): giving a person an insight into something that's happened to*

them, like watching snatches of the bonus DVD of their life

- *REWINDING (the strongest skill of all): the ability to stop time and unravel it back to a minute or so before*

I bet if I did that Woody would probably think I was showing him some text from a superhero graphic novel or an extract from a *Doctor Who* script.

'Hey, you know what they're like,' I say instead, giving a vague shrug.

'Spacey?' he suggests.

'Something like that,' I agree, even though I still don't totally understand what the angels are, even after all this time. Yes, we might be friends, but I'm too in awe of Sunshine, Kitt and Pearl to ask them such a personal question. Especially when I worry that I'm too simple and human to understand the answers.

'Are their parents as spacey?' asks Woody.

'*Foster* parents,' I correct him. 'No, they're pretty ordinary.'

Mr and Mrs Angelo are *very* ordinary – in the nicest way. They've fostered kids for years and years and have absolutely NO idea that the current bunch they're looking after arrived thanks to a trail of spells and spookdom.

'Anyway, we've got a meeting to go to, haven't we?' I say, giving Woody a playful nudge in the direction of Mr Edwards's ICT classroom.

We're due there now, along with the other members of the school-newsletter team. Woody nods and leads the way along another busy corridor, made narrow by a gaggle of students staring at something tacked up on the wall outside a music room.

'It's about the auditions tomorrow . . . for the Frost Fair,' explains Woody, squeezing by the small crowd. Without pausing, he cheekily taps the right shoulder of someone in the group, while passing on their left.

It's a girl with a neat black bob. As she spins round, I realize that:

a) it's Marnie Reynolds, and

b) thanks to Woody's trick, she's come face-to-face with *me* instead of Woody.

'It was him!' I say quickly.

I don't know Marnie that well. I mean, I did go to her (disastrous) party a few weeks ago, but that was just cos Kitt planted the idea to invite me in Marnie's head, not because she actually likes me or anything.

'It was her!' Woody jokes, pointing back at me.

Marnie's stern expression softens and she rolls her eyes at Woody. He's in her class – she knows he's a total spoofer.

'Sorry,' I mutter to Marnie, then shove past Woody and hurry – pink-cheeked – to Mr Edwards's class.

(I can hear Woody sniggering behind me, the big dork.)

'Good to see you, guys. Welcome back!' says Mr Edwards, ushering us both into his room, where

Hannah and Daniel are already hunched at a computer. 'Just got to wait for Billy and Ceyda, and we'll all be here.'

As I shrug my blazer off, I'm vaguely aware of a sweet-sounding, old-fashioned song drifting along the corridor – from one of the music rooms, I suppose. Someone already rehearsing for the audition maybe?

'It's OK, Woody – just leave it like that till the others arrive,' Mr Edwards is saying.

Ah, Woody was about to close the door. I'm glad it's staying open; I can't make out what that tinkly song is, and I'm trying to tune in. Random notes are niggling in my head, nudging me to recognize them.

'So, started on the new issue already?' Woody asks, walking over to join Hannah and Daniel. He drops his bag on to the desk with an ominous clunk. I don't think he's quite used to carrying a laptop in there yet. The school gave it to him to help him with his coursework, since anyone who has dyslexia

tends to do better on keyboards and screens. I just hope they don't expect him to give it back in one piece . . .

(*What IS that tune?* I think again, slightly distracted.)

'Yeah. The January issues of magazines and newsletters always have a round-up of the previous year,' mutters Daniel, moving text around. 'Thought we might use *this* as the opener.'

He clicks on an image and expands it so we can clearly see that it's the photo I took of Mrs Sharma, my form teacher. Or at least Mrs Sharma *was* my form teacher till she went and practically had her baby on the site manager's office floor.

In the photo, Mrs Sharma has her tiny newborn daughter Raina in her arms and is gazing lovingly down at her.

'Yeah, it's good,' says Woody, nodding. 'It'd look better if she wasn't holding that big potato, though!'

'She's *cuddling* her *baby*, you idiot!' Hannah turns and snaps at Woody.

Poor Hannah hasn't quite got used to Woody's dumb sense of humour yet.

'Oh *yeah*!' says Woody, leaning in towards the screen and pretending to realize his mistake.

Meanwhile, I hover behind Daniel, staring too. But I find myself drifting away, half trying to place the faint snatches of the song I can hear, and half thinking about Dot and her goofy idea of New Year 'Wishes'.

You know, if my sort-of-stepsister was here right now, and I had another chance to answer, I'd tell her this: I wish I could feel as close to my mum as Mrs Sharma is to little Raina.

'Hi!' comes a boy's voice at the door, and we all turn to see our two missing *News Matters* reporters. Ceyda waves her hello, and Billy is about to shut the door behind him.

'Uh, can you maybe leave it open?' I ask him. 'I like the music.'

Billy pauses, looking confused, then sticks his head back out into the corridor.

'Am I going deaf?' he asks. 'I can't hear anything.'

Sure enough, the song has faded away.

'Doesn't matter,' I say, turning back to the image of Mrs Sharma and Raina on the screen.

My wish is a bit stupid, I know.

I mean, I was only a few months older than Raina is now when Mum died in the traffic accident. So the chances of my dumb New Year Wish coming true . . .

That's about as likely as looking up and seeing penguins and dodos flapping and swooping in the sky, isn't it?

The sugar-coated telling-off

Flop!

That's all I want to do. Thunder up these stairs and then collapse on my bed. Kick my school shoes off and lie there, arms outstretched, till teatime. (Which'll be soon – I'm pretty late home from school.)

First days of term always get me like this. All that concentrating is hard on a brain that's been on holiday for a fortnight.

Plus me and Woody and Danny and everyone got together after school and did a load of work on the latest newsletter. It'll go out next week, with a special report on the Frost Fair – me and Woody offered to cover it this Saturday.

As I take the steps two at a time, I realize I'm humming four random notes over and over again. I've been doing it ever since lunchtime, since I heard that snatch of a song drifting down the school corridor.

Aargh! Like a bad case of hiccups that won't go away, the tune just –

I stop dead at my bedroom door.

There are giggles coming from inside. *Two* sets of giggles.

One giggler is bound to be Dot.

The other will be her best friend, Coco, who comes to ours for a playdate so often it's like she *lives* here.

Blam!

With a big grin, I barge right in.

They both jump, just like I planned.

But, whoa . . . I'm totally taken aback when I see what they're up to.

All I can do is raise my eyebrows and stare hard at my little sort-of-stepsister and wait for an explanation.

But what explanation can there be for Dot and Coco pinging my pants at each other?!

'RILEY!' Dot exclaims, lowering the blue spotty knickers she was about to catapult at Coco.

(My floral-patterned knickers are dangling from Dot's shoulder. Looks like Coco nearly got a bullseye.)

'What are you *doing*?' I squeak, finding my voice at last, and stomping over to them.

'It was . . . it was an ACCIDENT!' Dot announces uselessly, as I grab my dangling underwear.

Coco nods.

'So you just "accidentally" came into my room without permission,' I say, hurriedly stuffing my pants back in the open drawer the girls stole them from. 'Then "accidentally" rummaged in here –' I

slam the drawer shut – 'and "accidentally" played with my . . . my stuff?'

Dot blinks up at me. I think she's a bit stunned.

I'm a bit stunned too. Stunned that Dot's been so thoughtless with my things, and stunned at how cross I am. I'm never usually cross with her – she's as cute as a bucketful of kittens.

I guess it's not just because of the pants – embarrassing as that is.

It's also because I keep my little photo album hidden away in my knicker drawer. My few precious pictures of Mum are in there, and Dot and Coco are too young to understand what they mean to me.

They might get fingerprints on Mum without meaning too, or laugh at some out-of-date fashion she's wearing, and I couldn't bear that.

My panicky wave of crossness makes me remember something else.

'*And* you've been using my nail varnish without asking, Dot, haven't you?'

Three things happen pretty quickly:

1. Dot says no, then hides her guilty hands behind her back.
2. Coco starts crying.
3. Dad's girlfriend, Hazel, appears at the bedroom door.

'What on EARTH is going on here?' she asks, walking in and straight away wrapping a comforting arm round Coco.

'Riley's being sort of shouty, Mummy,' says Dot, shuffling into Hazel's side – the one that doesn't have Coco cuddled into it.

'I heard,' says Hazel, frowning at me.

At *me*!

My cheeks are pink-hot with crossness and now a dollop of unfairness too.

'They were playing with my pants!'

As soon as I say it, I know how silly it sounds.

Hazel rolls her eyes at me. 'For goodness' sake, Riley, they're only five years old. And look how upset you've made Coco!'

With that, Hazel shuffles both girls out of my room, muttering something about cookies and hot chocolate.

I can't believe it . . . If I went rifling through Hazel's underwear drawer and then pinged her bras all over the place, she'd hardly reward me with drinks and snacks, would she?

I bang my bedroom door closed, kick my shoes off so hard they smack against the wall, and crumple down on to the bed.

Then I see her and instantly calm down . . .

Mum.

She's on my bedside table, in the pretty mirror-edged frame that the angels gave me for my birthday. She's standing on the top of Folly Hill with her arms outstretched, her eyes to the skies, and a smile a mile wide.

'Hi, Mum,' I say softly, managing a wobbly smile of my own.

I often wonder what it would be like to have her around. But right now I wonder what it would be

like to have a mum to stick up for you. (Dot doesn't know how lucky she is . . .)

Tugging the drawer open again, I rummage through the rumpus of rumpled knickers for my photo album. My fingers quickly find the cool plastic of its cover.

I pull it out, set it on my lap, and stare down at the small square album. In the middle, a smaller square has been cut out of the shiny white plastic, and through it Mum is smiling up at me.

'Am I anything like you?' I murmur to her, thinking I *must* remind the angels of their promise to help me find out more about Mum. Though at the moment they just seem so absorbed in seeking the next –

'Knock, knock?'

Dad's in the room before I know it, and before I get the chance to hide the album. OK, so he might have given me the photos I keep in here (he left them on my bed not so long ago, wrapped in

ribbon), but he finds it kind of hard to talk about Mum. Actually, make that totally *impossible*. It hurts him too much.

'Hi,' I say nervously, putting both hands over the album in my lap, in an effort to hide it.

'Don't worry – I'm not here to have a go at you,' says Dad, coming over and sitting down beside me.

Er . . . hold on. He thinks I look nervous cos I'm guilty of being mean to Dot and Coco?

'But Hazel did say you lost your temper with the girls just now, Riley.' Dad gives me a sorrowful smile, a meaningful stare and a pat on the hand.

And those three things add up to me feeling a big wave of crossness again.

I thought I could count on Dad to stick up for me. But instead he actually *is* here to give me a telling-off, even if he's trying to sugar-coat it.

'They were in my room, Dad! And Dot's been stealing my stuff!'

'Now, stealing is a harsh word, honey.'

He pats my hand again and I'm about to argue back, when I see his face fall and feel his fingers move mine aside.

'Oh . . .' he says quietly, forgetting to give me a hard time all of a sudden. 'So this is where you're keeping her photos?'

I move the other hand and let him see.

'Yes, it's the perfect size,' I tell him, opening it up with slightly trembling fingers. 'I've got all six of the photos you gave me in here.'

I hardly breathe, bracing myself for Dad to stand up and leave the room. It's happened before.

'I remember . . . *that* was taken on Whitsea beach,' Dad murmurs instead, as he stares at Mum's carefree, happy face, tendrils of wavy hair flapping in the summer breeze.

He turns the page.

'And *that* one was when we cycled along the old rail track.' Mum on a bike, in denim shorts and a loose white T-shirt.

'And *this* one was the day she opened the shop.' Mum in a flowery dress outside her new florist's – Annie's Posies – pails of flowers under each arm.

'Lady Grace's Lake, in the autumn.' Mum wrapped up snuggly in a coat that's as red as the berries in the tangle of bushes behind her.

'That's Annie with a chocolate cake she'd made for our anniversary,' says Dad, flipping the page and gazing at the misshapen brown blob on a plate. 'She always was a rotten cook!'

Then he laughed.

Dad *laughed*!

And, apart from that small miracle, I just found out something I never knew about my mum. Being a rubbish cook isn't the sort of detail that might seem remotely important to anyone else, but I love it – *love* it.

'Ah! Well, this one speaks for itself, doesn't it?' With his index finger, Dad strokes the photo of Mum sitting up in bed holding a tiny something that Woody would probably describe as a potato, but of course it's a newborn me.

Out of the blue, Dad leans over and kisses me gently on the forehead.

Wow.

This might just be one of the most incredible moments of my life. Dad has never, EVER spoken this much about Mum before. Hey, maybe this is the start of something, with Dad opening up to me more. Maybe my New Year Wish will come true, without me having to ask the angels for help in finding out about Mu–

'Hee, hee, hee!'

The most incredible moment disappears, like the pop of a delicate floaty bubble.

We're being watched. There's a face at the crack in the door, spying on us and sniggering.

I love Dot, I really do, but I don't need her interrupting us right now, not when –

Hold it right there . . .

'Dot!' I bark, stomping towards the door. 'That is NOT funny!'

'Yes, it is! Hee, hee, hee!' She giggles some more, then runs away before I can grab my Hello Kitty pants – which she's wearing as a HAT.

'Dad! *See?*' I say, turning back to him.

Great. Instead of sympathizing, Dad is grinning madly. 'It *is* pretty funny, Riley, you have to admit!'

'Actually, I don't,' I say sharply.

There're no random music notes noodling in my head any more, just a roaring red rage.

I rush out of my room, down the stairs, past Alastair in his 'dog' basket and hurtle out of the front door.

Only one thing will make me feel better right now, and that's having an angel on my side . . .

The question and the answer?

The tickle starts at the back of my knee.

I no sooner bend down to scratch it than it moves to the side of my neck.

And – eek! – now it's as if someone is tickling my waist!

'Hee, hee!'

More giggling, but this time the voice doesn't belong to my sort-of-stepsister *or* her little friend Coco.

For a start, it's coming from a *tree*.

I look up at the looming chestnut in Mr and Mrs Angelo's garden next door and see a pair of white-blonde plaits dangling over the wooden rail of the treehouse.

So the tickles were tingles of errant magic . . .

'Coming up?' asks Pearl.

My hands are on the steps of the ladder before she's finished asking.

I need to blow off steam after the pants incident just now (and the way Dad and Hazel reacted); hanging out with the angels is exactly what I want to do.

'Hey, *nice!*' I say, as I come out on to the platform and see Pearl armed with a long, heavy piece of orange fabric and a staple gun.

The angels' dog, Bee, is curled up happily on something green and stripy. I'm always surprised when I see him up here. How a large fuzzy dog can clamber up and down the ladder so easily always amazes me. I must tickle his tummy one day and see if there are buttons or poppers there; maybe he's actually a small person in a dog-suit. (Nothing would surprise me with the angels.)

'Sarah gave us all these old curtains to make the place cosy now it's winter,' says Pearl, talking about her foster mum.

Skinny, girlish Pearl delicately gathers the orange material into nicely shaped swathes, then thunks and clunks and staples them to the treehouse roof like a muscly builder.

THUNK!

'Where are the others?' I ask her, settling myself down cross-legged on a pile of cushions to watch her at work.

'Sunshine is with Sarah, at the supermarket –'

THUNK!

'– and Frank –'

THUNK!

'– asked Kitt to help him take some stuff to the recycling depot.'

'Just as well, or you'd be in trouble for tickling me!'

'Shh!' says Pearl. She lifts a finger to her lips, then quickly lowers it when she realizes she's using the hand that's holding the staple gun. (Pearl still gets

pretty muddled and kerfuffled over human habits and tics.)

But why is she shushing me? The angels might have beyond amazing powers, but I don't think Sunshine and Kitt will be able to hear me from the other side of town, will they?

I'm about to carry on the conversation, to ask Pearl if she actually *did* have something to do with Lauren and the chewing gum in assembly this morning, when Pearl suddenly drops the staple gun to the floor with a clatter.

'Ooh, you're all purple again, Riley,' she says, kneeling in front of me and laying her hands on the top of my head.

I haven't a chance to respond; the warmth starts straight away.

It's like the sensation of bathwater gently pouring over my head, my shoulders and down my back.

It's like being stroked by soft hands.

Like being draped in silk.

Like being dribbled in melted chocolate.

OK, so it might be difficult to find the right words for this skill, but words don't matter when you feel so good, when you feel all the crossness bottled up inside just burble and trickle away . . .

'Better?' asks Pearl, letting her hands rest back by her sides.

'Better,' I say, nodding.

And, with my head clear of noisy, negative clutter, a shiny, clear thought pops right in there.

It's out of my mouth before I know it. 'Can you help me find out more about my mum, like you and Sunshine and Kitt said you would?'

Pearl sits back on her heels and tilts her head, silent for a few seconds. It reminds me of those pauses that happen with news reporters on TV, when they're listening to the voice of the producer in their earpiece, advising them what to say next.

Whatever's going on, Bee takes it as a sign that it's cuddle o'clock, and comes over to flop down beside Pearl.

'There are things you'll come to know,' she says finally, as she begins to stroke Bee's head. What Pearl's just said came out serious and stilted – not much like giggly Pearl at all. It's as if she's reading something off a script, or as if someone really *is* whispering in her ear.

'Are Sunshine or Kitt telling you this?' I check with her.

Pearl looks flustered. 'Um, no! No, it's not them! It's –'

Another pause.

'It's just me!'

Now *I'm* flustered. Something is odd here – but then everything to do with the angels is odd.

'OK. So what things will I come to know?' I carry on, anxious for details. 'And when will I know them?'

Another pause.

'Soon.'

I wait for a moment or two, hoping Pearl will say more, but that's all she seems able to tell me.

52

Excitement and frustration tangle together in my tummy. I wonder if I should pester Pearl, *beg* her for answers, but I know deep down that it won't get me anywhere. Angels – as I've come to realize – work in very, *very* mysterious ways.

But, as we're here, just the two of us, maybe there's something *else* I can ask her about . . .

On the day of Marnie's party, Pearl was weak and worried, scared her skills were fading. Opening a silky blue square of material, she revealed nine stuttering, faltering, fading little globes the size of marbles.

I haven't seen them since. She's not likely to talk about them or show them to me in front of her sisters, so now's my chance to ask if they're stronger and shining brighter.

'Pearl,' I begin. 'How –'

'They're good, thanks,' she says quickly.

'Did you – did you just read my mind?' I ask, freaked to know she can see in here. Pearl knows she's not meant to peek unless she has my permission.

'Sorry,' she says, biting her lip while agitatedly scratching and ruffling Bee's ears. 'Didn't mean to see that. Or *that*.'

That what?! What else has she spotted?

Aargh! I bet I know. It's the question I've always wanted to ask the girls: what exactly are they?

I've seen their *real* being, of course. I have a photo of the angels on my pinboard, though no one knows it's them. To Dad, Hazel and Dot it's just a snap of the stone Angel statue with three spangling spots of light floating in front of it, specks of sun reflected on my camera lens . . .

So maybe my question is more about the angels' past. What *were* they, and *where* were they? Before they turned up as the foster daughters of Mr and Mrs Angelo, I mean.

My mind is chattering, and Pearl is blinking, listening.

'Do you understand?' I say out loud.

'Um, no,' she admits, ruffling Bee's ears all the more madly.

Uh-oh. It's as if I'd just asked Pearl something that's impossible to answer, like, *What does yellow taste like?* Or: *How many sixes are there in a carrot?*

I try again.

'Before you were here, before you were a trainee angel, you must have been something else, somewhere else?'

Then I see her lips moving, but no sound is coming out. It's the quiet words: the way the girls communicate with each other, without being heard.

I might not be an angel – I might not have their skills – but I'm getting good at lip-reading.

'Someone could be listening,' Pearl says in silence.

I play her game and don't answer aloud. Has Pearl heard or sensed someone coming? I lift a flap of fabric and peek down below.

There's no one. Not a soul in the garden of number thirty-three, no one in my garden next door, nobody walking by on Chestnut Crescent.

I turn back to Pearl, but our cosy curtained cave is different. Very different.

I'm in a cocoon of glowing brightness, a glow like a silver sun shimmering around me.

Pearl sits still as the statue of Folly Hill, with her eyes transformed into two pools of pure light.

'Tell me, Pearl!' I urge her.

'I liked the breeze . . .' she murmurs, smiling at some vision only she can sense. 'I twirled and I twirled and I *twirled*!'

I hold my breath, waiting for the astounding, brain-exploding description that comes next.

I hold it for quite a long time, and then some more.

I hold it till I realize that's *all* the explanation Pearl has for me.

I also realize that she's so lost in this moment of random memory that she's been clutching poor Bee too tightly. It might have started out as a nice ear scratch, but now he's whimpering, his front paw flailing, trying to release the grip she has on either side of his poor head.

'Pearl! PEARL!' I say with urgency, giving her shoulders a shake.

The light pours away, her hands loosen and Pearl gives a shy girlish giggle.

Just in time – I can hear the crunch of gravel as one or other of her foster parents and sisters arrives back.

'Did that help?' her lips move and ask me.

'Sort of,' I lie, as discombobulated as Bee, who's now frantically scratching a freed fluffy white ear with his back leg.

So Pearl's explanation made as much sense as how many sixes are in a carrot, but finally asking the question *has* made me feel braver.

Watch out, Kitt – I'm going to ask *you* next . . .

Spot the catch

'Whoop! Whoop! Go, Marnie! Go, Marnie!'

Woody stands up and punches the air.

You'd think it was a sunny weekend afternoon and he was at some crowded stadium in America watching a baseball game.

Me, Sunshine, Kitt and Pearl sit still.

We know it's a rainy Wednesday lunchtime in the UK, and we're in the mostly empty school hall waiting for not many people to audition for the Frost Fair event.

Marnie is first up. (The other five or six students

here look knuckle-white with nerves, and they were happy for her to go ahead of them.)

As she walks up the stairs to the stage, Marnie gives Woody a long, cool look, which is hard to read. *Does she find his whooping funny, encouraging or annoying?* I wonder.

'Thank you for your enthusiasm, Woody!' Mr Hamdi, the head of music, booms through the microphone. 'Though I'm not sure "Whoop, whoop" is *entirely* appropriate given the type of music we're going for.'

Woody grins up at Mr Hamdi and, with a shrug, sits down next to me.

'The music's all got to be dead old-fashioned sounding cos of when the Frost Fairs took place,' Woody tells me, like I haven't figured that out already. We've both been doing plenty of research for our newsletter feature.

'Yeah, I don't think they were so keen on pop and rap hundreds of years ago,' I joke with him.

(Like I say, Woody's a dork, but kind of fun to dork around with.)

'Check THIS out,' Woody says, shaking his laptop out of the bag at his feet. He flips the lid and a website pops up. 'The first Frost Fair was held on the River Thames when it froze over in 1608, and the last one in London was held in 1814 – when an *elephant* was paraded up and down on the frozen river! How amazing is *that*?'

'Hope you're not expecting any elephants on Saturday,' I reply, holding my camera up ready. I've spotted that Marnie has taken her flute out of its case and is about to begin.

'So, Marnie, what piece are you going to be playing for us to–'

Mr Hamdi's words are drowned out in a sudden slip-slapping stampette of black ballet-pumped feet.

'Hello! Hi! Sorry we're late!' says Lauren, leading the way through the swinging hall doors with Joelle and Nancy following her like schoolgirl security

guards. 'Mr Hamdi, could I ask a favour, please? Could me and my friends audition first?'

'Well, *no*,' Mr Hamdi tells them, a little taken aback. 'Marnie's about to start and there are more people before you. You girls will just have to wait your tur–'

'But, Mr Hamdi, Joelle's got to leave really soon for a dentist appointment . . .'

Lauren sounds super-convincing – Joelle doesn't.

'Yeah, I've got this . . . uh . . . tooth thing.'

I bet it's not true; I bet Lauren's made it up on the spot. She just doesn't want to bother hanging around with the rest of us.

'Well, I –'

'Oh, *please*, Mr Hamdi!' Lauren simpers, in the voice she always uses to get round teachers. 'And Marnie doesn't mind. Do you, Marnie?'

Marnie raises her hands in a wordless 'whatever' and steps back from the mic.

'Right, I suppose *maybe* . . .'

Mr Hamdi doesn't get to finish what he's saying

because Lauren's already slip-slapping up the stairs to the stage, her sidekicks in tow.

Wow, Lauren's attitude *sucks*. She honestly makes my blood boil and my teeth grind.

And I'm guessing it's also made the haze of purple appear around my head, cos Kitt is giving me one of her hard stares – which is kind of freaky, even if she is my friend.

Whenever Pearl gazes at me, it's with eyes that are full of curiosity. Sunshine's eyes brim over with smiles and kindness. Kitt just stares, as if her eyes are scanning you inside and out, like a girl-shaped X-ray machine.

'Don't worry, Riley,' I read her lips saying. 'Very soon, you'll feel happy again.'

What does she mean? Is this a *catch*? It's Kitt's best skill: seeing just round the corner into the future, a glimpse of what might happen in the next few minutes.

Or is Kitt about to do some errant magic, same as she did on the school trip? Hey, maybe it *was* her

yesterday, when Lauren ended up in her gum-and-hair tangle? Maybe Kitt is getting better at hiding her guilt when she's used her powers the wrong way . . .

'One, two, three!' Lauren counts in professionally, taking the mic out of its stand.

Joelle and Nancy are positioned either side of her, heads down. They've all kicked off their pumps, I notice.

Why?!

'*All the single ladies!*' Lauren suddenly calls out.

At that first line of Beyoncé's hit song, the three girls break into a dance routine that they've obviously practised a LOT in each other's bedrooms, while Lauren sings the tune.

I feel my jaw drop and I watch, transfixed. Then I suddenly remember my job as the *News Matters* photographer and lift my camera up to record what's happening.

'Wow,' Woody mutters out of the corner of his mouth. 'They are truly, truly *bad*.'

They sure are.

Lauren is pouting and posturing so much that she doesn't seem to have noticed she's sliding through lots of different key changes where there shouldn't be any.

Joelle is strutting and jerking, unaware she looks like a mean and moody dancing chicken.

Nancy is the only one who seems uncertain; she's blushing fit to burst, her shoulders hunched as if she wants to fold herself up and disappear.

I shoot a sideways glance at Kitt, who's staring at the stage, her face still and unreadable.

Has she done this? Messed with their singing and dancing just enough to cheer me up? Well, it *has* cheered me up, but the slightly tuneless singing and the chicken dancing doesn't *really* have the sparkle of errant magic about it . . .

'Um, girls, girls,' says Mr Hamdi, wincing at some of the hip-wiggling, and holding his hands up to get Lauren and her buddies to stop. 'That's . . . quite something. But it's not what I'm after for the Frost Fair, I'm afraid. Didn't you read the posters?

We were expecting students to perform classical music, or at least music from the past.'

'But that Beyoncé track *is* from the past!' Lauren protests. 'It's ancient – it was a hit back in 2008!'

'It's not exactly what I meant,' says Mr Hamdi.

'Well, I told Marnie what we were going to do, and she said Beyoncé would be fine!' Lauren insists.

'Um, I think you and Marnie might have got your wires crossed. Modern songs like –'

'Sorry – Joelle's dentist thing,' Lauren interrupts Mr Hamdi, and she's gone, with her black ballet pumps in her hand and a glower for Marnie.

Marnie does another 'whatever' shrug in reply. And I'm sure I spot the tiniest twitch of a smile there too.

Both the shrug and sort-of-smile make me suddenly sure of three things:

1) Kitt did a catch, not errant magic.
2) Marnie deliberately let Lauren and her friends make fools of themselves.

3) Marnie Reynolds doesn't much like Lauren Mayhew. Which means *I* like Marnie a lot more than I did a couple of minutes ago . . .

'Right, can we get back to business?' says Mr Hamdi, ushering Marnie towards the mic. 'I hope you're not going to play any R&B hits, are you, Marnie?'

'No!' Marnie laughs, twirling her flute in her hand. 'I'm going to do "Greensleeves".'

I know 'Greensleeves'; it's from Tudor times. We listened to it in primary school when we were learning about horrible Henry VIII being mostly mean to his six wives. I remember Keira Cochrane playing it on her recorder for the class.

Back then, Keira just sort of *parped* the tune, *mostly* hitting the right notes. It's a different story with Marnie . . . I don't know anything about classical music but, watching Marnie, it's like we've turned on the telly and found ourselves watching some young flute genius on the Proms or something.

She's bobbing and weaving, doing these incredibly complex trills and swoops within the tune. It sounds *so* beautiful. So stunningly beautiful that it's making the hairs on the back of my arms prickle and tickle . . .

Hold on, I know that feeling. I've had it before, and it's *always* connected to the angels.

With a heart-lurch, I glance around quickly.

Uh-oh. My friends are totally and *completely* transfixed by Marnie's performance.

I just hope everyone *else* is too, because I don't need anyone in this hall spotting how intensely the girls are staring at the stage, how bright – how *unnaturally* bright – their eyes are.

Help! I'm not sure what it is about this centuries-old music but Sunshine, Kitt and Pearl are smiling, smitten, and so worryingly *lost* in the sound of it they might be in danger of giving themselves away any second.

'Kitt!' I hiss, nudging her hard with my elbow, trying to break the spell. 'Kitt!'

Kitt finally blinks, as if she's surfacing from a deep sleep and some wonderful dream.

And no, no, *no*! Now I've seen something that can't be happening.

It's Pearl –

Her shoulder blade under the navy of her blazer . . . it's quivering. There's only a small fluttering movement under the thick cloth, but a huge disaster is about to happen if I don't do something about it right *now*.

'Take this,' I turn and say under my breath to Woody, quickly handing him my camera.

'Where are you going?' he asks.

'Loo,' I mutter, as I stand up quickly, then reach out and grab Pearl by the elbow, dragging her with me to the swing doors.

I can see Mr Hamdi frowning at us from the stage. He probably thinks I'm being horribly rude. Instead, I'm just frantically worried.

Worried that Pearl is about to unfurl . . .

Sensing something . . .

Sunshine turns to glance over her shoulder.

Her red hair is pinned up on one side by those small multicoloured butterfly clips. The setting sun makes their plastic wing tips glint, as if they're moving, vibrating, about to take off and soar.

She's looking back at Pearl, checking on her.

'Is she all right?' I ask.

'She's fine,' Sunshine reassures me, turning round and carrying on walking. 'She's just tired and upset with herself.'

We're on the path by Lady Grace's Lake, and it's so narrow and overgrown that we're in pairs.

Me and Sunshine are leading the way, our gloved hands pushing stray springy branches away, our wellies stomping along in the scrubby earth and patches of soggy mud.

A little way behind us, Woody chats and jokes with Marnie. Scampering behind them are Dot and Bee – like a pair of puppy pals. At the back of our line are Kitt and Pearl, arm in arm, silent and thoughtful.

'Would she *really* have unfurled?' I whisper to Sunshine, now that I have the chance to ask.

Earlier today, outside the swing doors of the school hall, I'd thrown my arms round Pearl, pressing my hands down hard on her back, whispering an urgent, 'Stop, *stop*!'

In the bustling, crowded school corridor, I hoped the shuffling hordes of students might suppose that we were two giddy Year 7 girls hugging after having a falling-out.

To be honest, I didn't mind *what* they thought, as long as they didn't find out – or more importantly *see* – what was really going on.

And thankfully, locked in that hug with Pearl, I began to feel the flutter fade, the hint of the humps melt away and become simply skinny shoulder-blades again.

'I'm sorry, I'm sorry, I'm sorry . . .' Pearl had murmured in a panicky voice, as I led her back into the hall.

Afterwards, we hadn't been able to talk about what happened, the angels and me. There were bells and afternoon classes. There was Woody walking home with us, keen to talk about the Frost Fair and the newsletter, urging me to drop my schoolbag and head off to check out the lake together as background to our article.

And that's where we are now, though it's obviously not just the two of us here.

Woody had texted Marnie to meet us. 'Since she lives nearby,' he'd said.

I'm not sure how I feel about that, but I can hardly complain, since I've got all three angels, a five-year-old sort-of-stepsister and one and a half

dogs tagging along with me. (If you can count Alastair as half a dog.)

'Pearl *might* have realized and been able to stop herself,' says Sunshine, but she sounds more hopeful than convinced.

'Will she get . . . marked down for this?'

I'm thinking of the chart in the girls' airy white loft room, of course, where the nine angel skills are listed and each girl's efforts are marked on it. Pearl has an *awful* lot of black crosses.

And, more than that, I'm worried about the effect on Pearl's actual physical set of skills. Not that I can say that to Sunshine, in case she gets mad at Pearl for sharing her secret with me.

'Kitt and I failed too,' Sunshine suddenly surprises me by saying. Her perfect, pretty face has a frown framing it.

Wow, looks like Sunshine has too much on her own mind to go noseying into mine.

'What do you mean?' I ask.

'We all heard that beautiful sound and we let

72

ourselves be swept up in it. For a moment we all forgot what we were and why we're here. But Kitt and I are more . . .' Sunshine reaches for the right word, but either can't find it or doesn't want to say it. 'Kitt and I should have held back. We didn't look out for Pearl. So thank you, Riley, for helping.'

Sunshine puts a turquoise-gloved hand on my arm and I can feel a soothing coolness coming from the hand inside.

'That's OK. Of course I'll always help you all,' I tell her. 'If there's ever anything –'

Sunshine interrupts me. 'There is. Can you distract the others? We're sensing something . . .'

She looks me straight in the face, and I see that the peacock blues and greens of her irises are merging, moving, swirling. It's coming to them . . . the person they need to help next. I feel a shiver of excitement, thinking of the lucky person out there who's lost their shine, and who has no idea what's about to happen to them.

'OK, but don't be long – it's going to get dark soon.'

It was a stupid idea to come, really, since the days are short in January. But Woody had been so enthusiastic, so insistent. He'd said if we hurried we'd be able to look around the lake before the light faded. He'd persuaded me that if we took the tangly dog-walkers' route we'd quickly end up at the side that has been cleared and landscaped, ready for the Frost Fair on Saturday.

From there, we could come out on to Golf Road, with its bright street lights buzzing on, just as the sun began to dip away.

'We only need a few minutes,' Sunshine assures me. With that, she stops, pretending she has her glove stuck on a prickly twig, so that Woody, Marnie and Dot have to pass her.

'. . . and so I said, "Mum, you have GOT to be joking!"' Marnie is moaning. She and her mother don't get on, Woody told me. Marnie only had that disastrous party of hers to spite her mum for going away on a business trip. (Doesn't she know how grateful she should be to have a mum at *all*?)

'Hey, hold on! Where are THEY going?' says Dot, noticing that Sunshine, Kitt and Pearl are veering off down another path. And what's really bothering her, I can tell, is that Bee has trotted off with them.

I need to distract her. Now.

'Look, Dot! You can see the lake!' I say enthusiastically, pointing to the open glint of water up ahead.

'YAY!' she shrieks, and hurtles past me, Woody and Marnie. Behind her, Alastair bumps along on the muddy earth, dragged by his lead.

'Hey, race you!' shouts Woody, taking off after Dot.

Marnie, left behind, same as me, gives an awkward, shy laugh.

'I guess . . .' she says, tilting her head in the direction of the tall and small runners.

'We'd better catch them up?' I finish her sentence just as shyly.

Marnie gives another of her 'whatever' shrugs, same as she did on the stage earlier today. Then out of the blue she shouts, 'GO!'

As Marnie legs it, I hesitate for a second, grinning at her cheek. Then I begin to run after her, thinking all the while that I must ask her about the trick she played on Lauren today.

But my thoughts and my legs slow again as I hear a certain sound . . .

A tinkle of music. It's the same distant, sweet old-fashioned tune I heard in the ICT room yesterday. And, just like yesterday, I'm hearing it in snatches, so I can't make sense of it.

Where's it coming from?

Padding into the clearing, I see the small lake in front of me, its surface vivid, rippling shades of orange and mauve, reflecting the sun and darkening sky.

I see the cleared ground around it, free of dense

shrubbery and gnarled bushes, awaiting the tents and spectacle of the weekend.

I see Dot holding Alastair up for Woody to see/pat/talk to, and Marnie looking on with a smile.

I see all that, but I don't see anything or anywhere that could be connected to the song.

'Riley! Riley!' Dot calls out, racing towards me now, and the music slips away on the buffeting breeze. 'Alastair wants to give you a lick, Riley! HA, HA, HA!'

I frown at Alastair – then look at him harder.

'Wow, *that's* new!' I say, noticing that a dangling 'tongue' has been doodled on to his mouth.

'Arf!' Woody barks as he walks over, pulling a marker pen out of his jeans pocket.

'Isn't it so CUTE?' Dot giggles, obviously fine with Woody's teeny touch of graffiti. 'I LOVE IT! ARF, ARF, ARF!'

Then she's off, doing a flip-flappitty skip in her wellies, holding Alastair out in front of her and gazing at him in wonder.

'Wow, Woody – you're, like, Hillcrest Academy's answer to Banksy,' Marnie drawls, talking about the famous street artist. 'Only, you know, *rubbish*, obviously.'

'I'll graffiti YOU, if you're not careful, Marnie Reynolds!' Woody jokes back, whipping the top off his pen and threatening her with it.

'Don't you *dare*!' she shrieks.

'Just try to stop me!' he yells.

Grinning, I watch as they shriek, snigger and tussle, Woody trying to grab her, Marnie wriggling away from him.

Then I hear a sound, a splash that makes my heart freeze . . .

'Riley! Riley! HELP!' squeals Dot.

I kick off my wellies as I speed to her. She must've walked out along that little wooden jetty – I've only just noticed it now. She's up to her chest in the lake, and could go under any second, dragged down by the weight of her blue duffel coat.

'Swim to me, Dot!' I yelp, lunging into the cold

of the lake, my feet slipping and sliding on the mud underfoot.

Dot just bawls in reply, shock getting the better of her.

My gut-wrenching panic subsides when I realize Dot isn't in as much danger as I first thought. Here, at least, the lake is reasonably shallow. Water splashes and laps around my waist, and as I get to her, lifting her into my arms, I realize Dot must have been standing in the water, maybe on tiptoes in her wellies, with no real chance of drowning.

'It's OK, sweetie. I've got you,' I tell her, as she gratefully wraps her dripping arms and legs round me.

'Alastair! ALASTAIR!' she screams in my ear.

'Don't worry – Bee's got him,' I hear Woody say breathlessly. 'See, Dot?'

My dorky, wonderful friend is right next to me in the water, pointing towards the middle of the lake. I swivel Dot round, so she can see Bee swimming back to us, Alastair held tenderly in his jaws.

Then I hazily notice a flash of something disappearing under the water's surface near Bee: a stripy woollen scarf. Dot must have had it tucked under her coat, so I wouldn't see it. It was mine. A present in my Christmas stocking from Dad and Hazel . . . though that's not exactly important at a moment like this.

'Do you want me to take her?' Woody offers.

'No, it's all right,' I tell him, knowing that my shivering sort-of-stepsister is clinging to me so limpet-tight that she's not likely to let go till we reach dry land.

And on dry land is the welcoming committee: Marnie, Kitt and Pearl.

Sunshine is already gliding towards us through the water, and puts her hands on Dot's head as soon as she reaches us.

'Poor baby,' she mutters, as the healing warmth spills over Dot's head – unseen by the others but working almost instantly. Dot's shivering stops.

'My house is two minutes away,' Marnie calls

out, talking to us but pressing her mobile to her ear. 'I can lend you dry things and you can phone home and – Hello? Nan? Nan? It's Marnie. Can you make some hot chocolate or something? I'm at the lake – my friend's little sister fell in and she's really cold. No, it's OK. Honestly, she's not hurt or anything, just soaking wet and a bit shocked. We're coming now . . . Thanks!'

'Are *you* OK, Riley?' Woody checks with me, putting his hand on my back to help me up the bank of the lake with my heavy load.

'Mmm,' I mumble, not quite able to put how I feel into words.

The angels will understand, though. They'll sense my wildly thudding heart, the stress headache that's pounding in my brain and the awful, overwhelming knowledge that my little sort-of-stepsister could've died just now.

And so I look to them, at their three faces, their piercing blue eyes, for the understanding I know I'll find there.

But Sunshine, Kitt and Pearl are doing something totally unexpected.

They're *smiling*.

Smiling as brightly as if we'd just won a prize instead of nearly losing Dot.

I'm suddenly worried that these strange friends are even stranger than I thought . . .

Seeking, searching, finding

We walk into Marnie's flashy big kitchen and straight into an argument.

'What on *earth* are you doing that needs so much milk, Mum?' a clearly irritated woman's voice is asking.

'I'm making hot chocolate for Marnie and her friends!' a clearly irritated older woman's voice replies. 'She called five minutes ago to say Oh, here they are now!'

All of us hover in the extra-wide doorway between the hall and the kitchen. I think we're all a little wary, worried about interrupting.

'Oh, for goodness' sake, Marnie!' says the younger of the two women – Marnie's mum, obviously. They have the same olive skin and black hair, though Mrs Reynolds's is scraped back into a neat short ponytail. She's dressed in razor-sharp black trousers and a soft grey jersey that looks like it might be incredibly expensive.

'What?' says Marnie with a shrug and a frown. 'I haven't opened my mouth and I've done something wrong?'

I feel the tiniest shudder. At first I think it's Dot, who's holding my hand, shivering with cold. But this is a vibration I feel *inside* . . . I glance at the angels and see them staring wide-eyed, taking in the tense atmosphere.

'No offence to your friends –' Mrs Reynolds holds up a hand, making a gold bracelet jangle – 'but you can't go inviting people back here without giving me any warning, Marnie. I've got work to finish. I can't drop everything and suddenly rustle up tea for . . . for however many you all are!'

'Mum, I haven't brought them for tea! I already phoned and told Nan that –'

'Whoa, what's going on? What have you been doing?' Mrs Reynolds interrupts, looking behind us and spotting the trail of muddy footprints in the hallway. 'And can somebody stop the dog from making that mess?'

We all look down and see Bee shaking himself, doing the doggy quick-dry fix. At that same moment, a phone rings loudly in Mrs Reynolds's hand.

'No . . . not the office *again*!' she whines, sounding a lot like Dot when she's been told it's time to get the knots combed out of her hair.

'Penny – go and answer your phone. I've got this,' says Marnie's nan, gruffly ordering Mrs Reynolds out of the room with a wave of the spoon she's holding. She's wearing a bracelet too, but hers is made of colourful glass beads, which match her chunky necklace.

I've met Marnie's grandma before. She – amazingly, wonderfully – recognized me because I

looked like Mum. She knew her because she bought all her flowers from Annie's Posies. I might be wet, tired and emotional just now, but I'm also a little bit thrilled to be in her company again. I wonder if I can ask her some more about Mum . . . It might be quicker than waiting for the angels' help. (Yes, OK, so I'm still kind of cross and confused about their reaction back at the lake.)

'Right, gorgeous Annie's *equally* gorgeous daughter . . .' Marnie's nan turns to me with a cheerful smile. 'Can you remind me of your name, and tell me what happened to this little one of yours?'

I feel my cheeks flood scarlet. No one's called me gorgeous before. No one ever mentions my mum. I'm sure everyone is staring at me. But I don't care; hearing this woman say Mum's name out loud makes my mum feel instantly more real to me. I feel like running round the kitchen island and giving Marnie's nan a huge hug.

'I'm – I'm Riley,' I stammer. 'We were walking by the lake, and Dot went to the end of the jetty, and –'

'And my wellies tripped me up,' Dot finishes, gazing down at her wet socks. 'They're still stuck in the mud!'

'Serves them right! Naughty wellies,' jokes Marnie's nan, her eyes cartoon wide.

Everyone laughs – and stops paying attention to me and my flushed cheeks, which is a relief.

'Now, the rest of you, take off your muddy shoes and wellies and leave them by the door, my lovelies!' Marnie's nan carries on cheerfully, as she pours hot milk into waiting mugs.

Even her hair is cheerful. It's like puffed-up candyfloss.

'I'll sort the floor, Nan,' says Marnie, grabbing a mop from the cupboard in the hall.

'Good girl. Then your moany mum won't have anything to moan about!' Her nan laughs. 'And *you* look like a strong boy –' she's smiling at Woody, as he pads back into the kitchen in his wet socks – 'so could you carry this tray downstairs, please? We'll be *much* cosier there!'

Of course. Marnie's nan lives in the granny flat downstairs. I've never been inside it. I just saw the door to it when I was out in the garden during Marnie's party.

'Sure, Mrs . . . Mrs . . .' Woody stumbles.

'Etta. Please call me Etta. Here, I've looked out some clothes for those of you in need,' says the old woman, wandering round the vast, shiny kitchen island and holding a hand out to Dot. 'And I've got some lovely *medicinal* biscuits in my cupboard too!'

Dot might have been ashen-white with shock on the way here, but her face suddenly pinks at the mention of biscuits.

Five minutes later, I'm coming out of the granny-flat bathroom wearing a strange combination of flowery PJ bottoms and a slightly too-tight T-shirt with I LOVE CYPRUS! on it.

'Looking good!' Woody grins at me from the sofa. He can talk: Marnie's tracksuit bottoms stop right above his ankles.

'Don't you think my hoodie matches his eyes?' Marnie asks.

It's red.

Woody jumps up and begins to parade about, model-style, posing and pouting for all he's worth. Not that there's much space to parade; unlike the huge, stylish house upstairs, this place is practically doll-sized, and made smaller but cosier still with all the colourful clutter everywhere.

'Ooh, you're a proper supermodel!' says Etta, tilting her head back and laughing loudly.

She's on the sofa with Dot, who's curled up in a big hand-knitted jumper with her knees tucked inside. I think she must be on her zillionth biscuit.

The angels and Bee are all slouched on the fuzzy rug in front of the gas fire, where Sunshine is holding her bare feet to the heat. I wonder what strange thoughts are swirling around their unknowable minds. Before they came rushing at the sound of Dot's screams, had they figured out who needs their help? Actually, maybe *that* was

the reason for their matching smiles back at the lake . . .

'Riley, sit here!' says Etta, patting the space beside her where Woody had been sitting seconds before.

I do as I'm told and plonk myself down, taking the mug she's holding out to me.

'Thanks,' I say politely. 'So you've met Alastair, then?'

Dot's pet is nestled on her lap, like a wooden sausage dog.

'Oh, he's a lovely boy,' Etta coos, and gives him a stroke. 'So is Bee. I was just telling Dot about my darling Harry, who sadly passed away not so long ago . . .'

At this, Etta gazes up at the mantelpiece, which is stuffed with photos in silver frames. Some are of an elderly, smiley, grey-haired man who looks like he might be Greek Cypriot, and some are of a black-and-white spaniel.

I'm not sure which one is Harry.

There's certainly no sign of either an elderly man or a spaniel here in the flat.

'He was such a sweetheart. The love of my life.'

So Harry's her husband.

'My George loved him too . . . always out for walks together. George used to say, "Harry, lead!" and Harry would lollop off and grab it from the hall table in our old house and –'

Wait, no – Harry's the *dog*. And George is – was? – her husband.

As Etta chats away about her beloved pooch, I notice that, while her voice is bright and her smile wide, her eyes are filling up with tears. Uh-oh. I'm suddenly worried that she might cry in front of us. Which could be upsetting for her, since we're all strangers, except for Marnie.

Hold on. I'm friends with three girls whose job it is to sense emotions.

I look down at Sunshine, Kitt and Pearl to gauge their reactions, and see something in their faces that *instantly* explains the smiles by the lake.

That same beatific, mysterious smile is on each of their faces as they listen to Etta talking. Wow . . . the sisters have found who they've been looking for, haven't they?

The seeking and searching is over.

They've found Etta!

But why do they think she is so in need of –

'Hello – Riley?' says Mrs Reynolds, after tapping on the door but walking straight in.

'Yes, that's me!' I reply, since Marnie's mum doesn't know which girl here owns my name.

'Your dad's here.'

Ah, yeah. I phoned him at work, while we were walking to Marnie's, and asked him to pick us up when he finished at the print shop.

'Great!' I say, though I wish he'd arrived just a few minutes later, so I could study Sunshine, Kitt and Pearl a little more, and figure out what might be going so wrong in Etta's life that their search has ended with her.

'Dotty, are you all right, my darling?'

Oh, it's Hazel too, coming rushing into the room and scooping a startled Dot up off the sofa and into her arms.

'I can't believe I could've lost you!' Hazel is muttering, holding my little sort-of-stepsister so tight that the biscuit she's been holding crumbles in her hand.

'She's all right,' I reassure Hazel. 'The water wasn't that deep.'

'But it *could* have been!' says Hazel.

The combination of those words, the sharp, stressed tone she uses to say them, and the glare she's just given me add up to one thing: Hazel blames me for not looking after Dot properly.

'Dad?' I appeal to him. 'Dot's OK – I went straight in, and Woody and the others all helped.'

Dad rubs his hands through his brown hair and his eyebrows furrow. I can see he's not a hundred per cent on my side either.

'Riley, sweetheart, why were you even at Lady Grace's Lake at this time of day?' he asks wearily,

pointing to the garden in shadows outside and the dark starry sky above.

That's not fair. It wasn't this dark when we were at the lake. And it's not even five o'clock now. He's making it sound like I took Dot out on a midnight stroll!

'We were researching for an article in the school newsletter,' I try to explain, nodding at Woody. 'It's about the Frost Fair that's happening this weekend. I did tell Hazel where we were going.'

'The washing machine was on!' Hazel snaps. 'All I heard was you saying you were going for a walk! I didn't expect –'

I don't hear the rest of Hazel's complaint.

'Thank you for your help,' Dad interrupts, directing his words to Mrs Reynolds and Etta. 'Come on, grab your things and let's go, kids.'

Interrupting Hazel, doling out brief thanks, handing out blunt orders . . . that's not Dad's usual way of talking *at all*. He's normally as soft and sweet as a teddy bear filled with fudge.

And what's made his face go as ashen-white as Dot's was when she fell in the lake?

I hear a murmur in my head. It's Sunshine using quiet words. What is it she's saying?

Then I suddenly figure it out, though it docsn't make any sense.

'*The Frost Fair . . .*'

Hold breath, cross fingers

I slept for about six minutes the whole night.

So this morning I turned over and curled into my cosy duvet, grateful that it was a lovely lazy Sunday.

Then my alarm went off and I realized that it was actually Thursday. A school day. Groan . . .

What had kept me awake and left me this tired? Questions and puzzles that'd whirled endlessly around my mind, nudging me every time I began to nod off.

Why was Dad completely thrown by the mention of the Frost Fair yesterday? Could it be a Mum thing? He'd had that same strained, sad look . . .

Why is Hazel always so cross with me at the moment? I don't think she's ever been that keen on me, but this feels different.

Why are the angels so sure that Etta – possibly the most bright and sparkly old lady I've ever met – has lost her shine and needs their help? On the way to school they told me they don't know yet; they need to spend more time with her. But – and here's another question – how's *that* going to happen?

When will I get the chance to be alone with Kitt and ask her where the angels came from? They stick together whenever they can.

What is with the weird snatch of music I've not-quite-been-hearing this week? It's freaking me out. Did I even hear it? Nobody else seemed to have . . .

And, speaking of music, why did the angels react to Marnie's flute piece so dramatically yesterday? Maybe because they were seeing her but sensing her connection to Etta?

But right now those questions and puzzles seem fuzzy and not that important. I'm so tired I could

put my head down on this desk and sleep, sleep, *sleeeeepppppp* . . .

Not that it's going to happen. Not when I'm in class, and not when Lauren Mayhew's cocky voice is ringing in my ears.

'I *still* don't see why they don't want cool music at the fair.'

Mr Hamdi tries to answer patiently. 'As I've said already, they want music that reflects the period when Frost Fairs were held, which is why Marnie Reynolds will be performing "Greensleeves". And I'm afraid that – "cool" as she is – Beyoncé wasn't a big hit in the seventeenth to eighteenth centuries . . .'

Joelle makes a disrespectful '*tsk*' noise in support of her friend, or Beyoncé, or both.

'The sort of music they want – especially from earlier in that period – can sound almost . . . almost *magical* to us now,' Mr Hamdi carries on, trying to steer the conversation away from pop hits. 'It really can leave you with a hairs-standing-up-on-the-back-of-your-neck sensation. Here, let me put this

on for you. It's called "Gaudete". It's known as an ancient sacred song, and . . . now, where is it?'

Lauren bangs her head – or at least *mimes* banging her head – on the table three times. She does it behind Mr Hamdi's back, of course, while he's frowning at the screen of his laptop. And then it starts . . . no intro, just harmonizing voices singing straight away.

Like Mr Hamdi, I try closing my eyes.

And suddenly the music really is other-worldly, a hundred thousand light years away from our fluorescent-lit chrome-and-plastic classroom.

A strangely beautiful sound that seems to stretch all the way back to medieval times.

And it's a sound that's being spoiled by sniggering.

Opening my eyes, I see Lauren, Joelle and Nancy giggling and mugging along to the song. Worse still, it's started a low-level Mexican wave of silliness around the room.

Mr Hamdi hasn't noticed yet, cos he's closest to the speakers, but he will as the sniggering swells.

And then we'll probably all end up with a group detention, thanks to stupid Lauren May–

Then something happens.

A new sound happens.

A new sound that immediately gives me that eerie, hairs-standing-up-on-the-back-of-my-neck sensation Mr Hamdi talked about.

The angels are singing. Singing along to 'Gaudete', with overlapping voices so pure and perfect that I can practically feel the shock in the room all around me.

Mr Hamdi's eyes open wide in surprise, his mouth drops.

Please, no! I think in a panic, turning to look at Sunshine, Kitt and Pearl for signs of strangely brightening eyes or hidden wings emerging.

There's nothing, luckily. Just three heads held high, faces radiating happiness as they sing.

But I almost feel I need to hold my breath, to cross my fingers tight, to *will* my friends not to show themselves for who they really are.

And so when the song ends, and I can finally breathe again, I slump, weirdly exhausted.

There's a second of stunned silence, then Mr Hamdi starts clapping madly, and everyone joins in, even Joelle and Nancy. (Lauren looks gobsmacked, but can't bring herself to be nice.)

'Girls! Girls! That was stupendous!' he says once the frantic applause has died down. 'Why didn't you tell me you could sing like that?'

'We didn't know we c—'

'We were too shy,' Kitt says over Pearl's words, sounding more stern than shy.

She's lying, of course. But Kitt knows her shy lie is more believable than Pearl's honesty.

'Well, you'd better get over your shyness, ladies,' says Mr Hamdi, 'because you HAVE to perform at the Frost Fair now!'

'We'd love to,' Sunshine replies with a serene smile.

And then she says something else, but just to me.

'Thank you . . .' her quiet words whisper softly in my head.

'Why did you thank me?' I ask Sunshine, as class spills out in a jumble of people, bags and chatting.

Sunshine smiles at me, but I have the funniest feeling she's using the smile to give herself time to think . . .

'Hey, there's Marnie,' Pearl suddenly pipes up excitedly, pointing at the squash of people milling around in the corridor. 'We have to talk to her. We have to tell her we need to be friends with her grandmother!'

'It doesn't work like that, Pearl,' says Sunshine, turning her attention away from my question. 'Does it, Riley?'

'Well, no,' I reply. 'Young people and older people aren't friends exactly.'

'They're enemies?' Kitt asks, her dark brows frowning over the top of her black glasses.

The angels have slotted into the human world incredibly well, but every now and then they need me to translate. Sometimes I fail; they still don't understand the point of random things like ties, shaking hands or people being afraid of birds. But then, neither do I.

'No. I didn't mean that,' I say hurriedly. 'What I mean is . . .'

My explanation slithers away as Marnie comes closer. I've just had an idea.

'Hey, Marnie – guess what?' I call out to her.

'What?' she asks, sidestepping some running boys so she can safely join us.

'Sunshine, Kitt and Pearl just sang something for Mr Hamdi, and he says they *have* to perform at the Frost Fair!' I tell her.

'Yeah?' she says, smiling round at my friends. 'What did you sing?'

'We don't know!' Pearl says with a little laugh.

'She's forgotten the name,' Sunshine slips in quickly to cover up for her sister. 'It was . . .'

Uh-oh. The angels have no idea of the song's title, or why that unheard piece of music chimed with them so much.

'It was called "Gaudete",' I chip in swiftly.

'Oh, I know that!' says Marnie, her face lighting up. 'It's really pretty.'

OK, this idea of mine is working well so far. And the angels have just figured out that I'm going somewhere with this. Their eyes are all on me; I can feel it.

'Well, if you guys are *all* performing on Saturday, why don't you have a rehearsal together sometime?' I suggest, as if it had only just occurred to me.

Small pleased smiles break on Sunshine, Kitt and Pearl's faces.

'That would be great!' says Marnie. 'But it's Thursday already, and the Frost Fair is on Saturday, so –'

'So we could come round to yours after school

today?' says Sunshine, stepping in now she can see what I've started.

'Today?' Marnie wonders aloud. 'Um, yeah . . . today would be OK. Or I could come to yours?'

'No,' Kitt says, in her sometimes too-blunt manner.

Marnie's face falls a little.

'She means we'll come to your house,' Pearl butts in with a beaming smile.

Marnie's frown lifts slightly.

'Your house is bigger,' says Sunshine.

'Better acoustics,' I add.

Marnie blinks, smiles and nods. 'OK, see you after school!'

As she walks off, her sharp shiny bob swinging, I feel three hands rest on my back, as if the owners of the hands were quietly reassuring me that I did the right thing, a good thing.

I appreciate the gesture. Even though I know that, to anyone passing, the angels aren't touching me at all . . .

The story of the lost shine ...

Apparently angels find school uniforms as annoying as human kids do. Who knew?

That's why we've arranged to go home and change before we set off to Marnie's.

(Officially, I'm tagging along, cos I'm the *News Matters* photographer and I'll snap the girls' rehearsal. Unofficially, the angels aren't going *anywhere* without me.)

I kicked my shoes off down by Alastair's basket just now (he didn't wake up), and I'm pitter-pattering upstairs, wriggling out of my blazer already and thinking what I'll wear if my jeans aren't washed yet. Maybe my shorts and woolly tights . . .

But then outfits go out of my mind as I reach the top landing and hear giggles.

Dot and Coco, of course.

Luckily, however, the giggling *isn't* coming from my room this time.

I pause by Dot's door and listen. I love eavesdropping on Dot and Coco. They have the craziest conversations ('Do you think there are naughty unicorns?') and make up the weirdest games ('You be the baby and I'll be the mummy penguin!').

What are they up to now?

Actually, the bedroom door is open just a crack, enough to spy – in the nicest way – on my little sort-of-stepsister.

Ha! Dot's wearing a big beach towel round her shoulders, as if it's a cape.

'I want you to be a good girl today and learn ALL your spells, Hermione. OK?'

'OK!' Coco giggles.

Cute. They must be playing a Harry Potter game.

'THESE are the spells we are going to do today,' Dot announces in what I think is supposed to be a posh voice. She has a scruffy-looking bit of paper in her hand. 'FIRST, we will do *s-ee-k-in-g*,' she says, trying her best to spell out the letter sounds. 'What's that? Seek-*ing*? Then . . . uh . . . *something w-o-r-d-s*. That spells "words"!'

My blood runs icy-lake cold as Dot deciphers what's on the note. Is she talking about quiet words?

'Er, the next one is WAY too hard for me to read,' she blithely carries on. 'So we won't do that one.'

Virtual stroking: what the angels did earlier, placing their hands on my back . . .

'This one is *w-ar-m-th* . . . That's *warm-th*! And the NEXT one . . .'

The next one is springing, and it's followed by catching, spirit-lifting, telling and rewinding. But Dot's not going to get to those.

I've stood statue-still in shock for the last couple

of seconds, but now I leap into the room and grab the piece of paper out of Dot's hand. I'm shaking. She has the list of all nine skills and what they are. But I got rid of it; I scrunched it up and threw it in the bin in my bedroom.

'What are you doing with this? It's mine!' I snap at her.

'You said it was just silly writing! You said it was rubbish!'

I did. When Dot skipped into my room a few weeks ago and nosied at my notepad, I'd come up with the first lie I could think of and told her it was an idea for a creative-writing project.

'Dot, even if I said it was rubbish, it doesn't mean you can help yourself to it!'

'But it was in your BIN!' Dot argues.

'Even if something's in my bin, that's *still* stealing!'

'Oh for goodness' sake, not again!' Hazel's voice bursts into the argument. '*Now* what?'

Urgh . . . In a repeat of Tuesday, Coco is crying

and Hazel ends up with two small girls snuggling into her sides for protection.

'Dot took something that belonged to me,' I try to explain.

'It was just a TEENY bit of paper from her bin!' Dot insists, holding up her finger and thumb and making a tiny space. 'It was all scrunched up. She'd thrown it away!'

Hazel says nothing – she just gives me a look that very clearly means I'm a big disappointment. That I'm a useless sort-of-stepsister.

There's no point in arguing, so I turn and head towards my own room, muttering, 'I'm going out in a minute.'

'Sorry, you can't,' Hazel tells me, sounding harassed. 'You'll have to stay with these two. I'm already late for my shift at the hospital and your dad is stuck in traffic and running late.'

I'm about to blurt, 'That's not fair!' but then I decide to be smarter than that . . .

*

'Welcome to my life . . .' groans Marnie.

Once again, we've walked into her flashy big kitchen and straight into ANOTHER argument. I'd avoided the one with Hazel by just saying OK to babysitting Dot and Coco, then telling the girls to get their coats on as soon as she left. Don't know if Dad will be home yet but I've left a note for him.

'Does this happen a lot?' I murmur to Marnie.

'Oh yes, ever since Nan moved in downstairs,' she says with a sigh while the fight rages on.

'For goodness' sake, why have you moved everything around, Mum?' Mrs Reynolds is sniping at Etta, as she opens glossy cupboard doors, then slams them shut.

'Because I was trying to *help*!' Etta is sniping back.

'Do you two *have* to do this?' asks Marnie, as she goes and grabs a carton of orange juice out of the fridge for us. 'I have friends here, if you haven't noticed!'

How funny – it's as if Marnie has a mute button

on. Her mum and nan pay her no attention and keep narking at each other.

'Well, I don't find it very helpful not knowing where everything is, actually!'

This is *so* uncomfortable. I wish I could slink off and join Dot and Coco, who we've parked in the giant playroom in front of the ginormous TV.

'And there I was, thinking I was doing something nice for you, Penny!' says Etta, folding her arms across her ample chest.

It's hard to read what Sunshine, Kitt and Pearl make of all this. Their faces are expressionless, but their eyes are glued to Etta and Mrs Reynolds. It's as if they're watching a wildlife documentary or something. Even Bee is staring at them, with who knows what going through his doggy mind.

'*Nice* would be just leaving things where they are, instead of confusing everyone,' growls Mrs Reynolds, finally laying her hands on the packet of coffee she must have been looking for.

'Well, excuse me for breathing!' snaps Etta.

'Stop it, stop it, *stop* it,' Marnie is hissing as she clunks glasses on to a tray.

'Oh, Mum! Don't be so dramatic!' says Mrs Reynolds, rattling noisily around in a drawer for something or other.

'Dramatic? Well, that's grateful! You're always so busy, Penny, and I have nothing to do, so all I –'

'Well, maybe you should find something to do in your *own* flat,' Mrs Reynolds interrupts, 'instead of coming up here and interfering with our things!'

'Thanks a lot, Penny,' says Etta, and she starts walking off. 'I know when I'm not wanted!'

And then it begins . . . tiny tremors, a hardly heard hiss of vibration, a faint flicker of the lights. The angels are at work, stopping this situation in its tracks. They came here to be closer to Etta, and the last thing they want is for her to storm out.

Which skill are they using? I wonder.

OK, I can see it's virtual stroking. Etta's shoulders sink and relax, her steps slow. The pinched look

leaves Mrs Reynolds's face. Even the harsh overhead lights seem to soften from a cold mauve-ish to warm yellow.

'Sorry, Mum,' says Mrs Reynolds. 'Work's getting me down. Didn't mean to snap.'

'I know, Penny. You get back to your office, and I'll make your coffee and bring it through when it's ready.'

As Mrs Reynolds nods her thanks and goes off, Marnie seems speechless, hardly believing what she's just seen and heard.

It's Sunshine who talks next. 'We came to rehearse for the Frost Fair. Would you like to hear us?' she asks Etta.

'Yes, I would! I'd like that very much,' comes the reply, Etta clapping her hands together. 'Shall we do it right now? The coffee can wait a few minutes, I'm sure . . .'

She gives us a cheeky wink, and waves us to follow her through to the living room.

'Oh . . . I thought my flute case was in my

schoolbag,' mutters Marnie. 'It must be in my room. Back in a minute!'

I spot a glint in Sunshine's eyes. Has Marnie's flute been magicked elsewhere for a reason? A reason like getting Etta on her own? I feel a flutter of excitement about what might come next, and then a pang of envy too. Every bit of the angels' energy is focused on Etta. Now that she's their new project, there'll definitely be no time to help me find out more about Mum . . .

'So are you singing or playing something, Riley, dear?' Etta asks me as she plonks down on one of the two squashy sofas, with Bee settling himself at her feet. The angels kneel down next to him on the plush, vintage patterned rug.

'Oh, I'm just here to take photos. For the school newsletter,' I explain, sitting down next to Marnie's nan.

'What, with *that*?' she laughs, pointing at my lap.

Oops – I'd forgotten I was clutching Alastair. Dot had insisted on bringing him today, then

dumped him on me when she and Coco decided to play don't-step-on-the-cracks on the way here. (They'd bounced along the pavement like a pair of crazy frogs.)

'Oh yeah,' I say with a smile, trying to rummage in my bag for my camera and not really knowing where to put Alastair.

'Here, let me,' says Etta, taking the log dog and settling it in her own lap. 'Who's a lovely boy, then? And you too, of course . . .'

Etta strokes Alastair's 'back' with one hand, while reaching down to ruffle Bee's ears.

Spotting their moment, the angels make their move.

Pearl leans against Kitt, while Kitt rests one crossed knee up against Sunshine's, and Sunshine reaches out and places her hand on Bee's head too, so that her fingers 'accidentally' brush Etta's.

Instantly Etta's eyes mist over, as if she's been hypnotized. Which she has, obviously.

They're about to spring her, to find out why

this lovely, friendly lady has deep down lost her shine.

I hope Marnie's search for her 'missing' flute case lasts long enough for her nan's story to be told, I think while glancing quickly in the direction of the stairs. (My crossed fingers might not be as powerful as the angels' magic, but it's the best I can do.)

'Oh, I miss my house . . .' I hear Etta say, and a sweet, sad smile plays at her lips. 'But how could I stay there? Only me and all those empty rooms . . .'

She's sad about leaving her old home. So that's the story of her lost shine. Of course.

'All those years there . . . how many times did we decorate? George always grumbling, up a ladder with a paintbrush. Ha! And his relatives coming from Cyprus. All the cooking he'd do! The smell of the food . . .'

Etta's eyes close and she takes a deep breath, as if she can smell the herbs and spices.

'And Penny . . . such a sweet baby. But so independent! Never liked cuddles . . . The only

times we've really hugged was when her divorce happened, and when her dad died. Oh, George . . .'

Sunshine slides her hand across Etta's to help to soften the sadness. Leaving her house and losing her husband – together they're the reasons why Etta is so blue.

'But it was almost a blessing, wasn't it, George? You were so poorly you wanted to go . . . Harry wouldn't leave your side. Harry . . . such a darling. Such a comfort. Looking into his brown eyes was like looking into yours, George . . . And then, and then . . .'

Etta's eyes fill with tears and I panic. Is this the right thing to do? To make her upset? Automatically I reach out and touch her arm – and then I sense a little of what's happening to her.

It's like being in a deep, warm bath, so deep it's as if she's floating. It's calm and safe and she can say anything she wants to.

'You know what hurts? I can't tell anyone that Harry dying was almost worse . . .'

Bee shuffles upright and plants his head in her lap, practically nose to nose with Alastair. His pale-as-water eyes gaze up soulfully at Etta. Don't they always say that dogs can sense emotions?

'People don't understand that it was because Harry was my link to you, George . . . When Harry went, it felt as if *you* were finally . . . finally gone . . .'

As her words trail off, I hear someone say something.

'*Spirit-lift,*' Sunshine whispers silently to her sisters, and to me, and it begins.

Etta looks up, smiling as she moves around the memory they're replaying for her.

It's Etta laughing delightedly, as her George places a wriggling bundle of puppy in her lap. In her mind, she reaches out to cuddle it. And here on the sofa she does the same, only her hands are stroking Alastair.

Alastair . . .

Uh-oh! I let go of Etta's arm, so I know what I'm seeing is real, and not a spirit-lift memory.

Bee is whining, delightedly licking Alastair's face. And Alastair has just licked him *back*!

'Sunshine!' I say urgently to the most experienced of the angels.

All three girls' eyes are shining silver, but start to fade at the sound of my voice.

And then they see what I see. A long brown puppy – tail wagging, tongue dangling – is wriggling to life on Etta's lap. Alastair's hard surface is turning soft and shiny with fur.

This is all wrong! It's errant magic, which shouldn't be happening . . .

a) at all, and

b) because I just heard Marnie's bedroom door slam. She's on her way down!

Sunshine looks shocked.

'It wasn't me!' Pearl says quickly.

'Or me,' Kitt adds.

'Hands . . . everyone, *now*!' Sunshine orders,

ignoring the question of who did the errant magic and concentrating on finding a way to get us out of this mess. 'Riley – you too.'

I don't think; I just do as she says.

Together, forty fingers press down on Alastair, and between the space of one blink and another he's transformed back into a stiff, lifeless hunk of driftwood.

'Got it!' Marnie calls out, as she trots into the living room holding her flute case aloft. 'It was in my bag after all! Don't know how I missed it.'

She's also missed the four of us leaping away from Etta and back into our former positions. I glance at my friends, and flash them a smile of relief. We did it!

'Yes, we did,' I hear Sunshine reply in quiet words. She's allowing herself a small smile too, same as Kitt. Pearl gives a nervous little giggle, and slaps her hand across her mouth, in case Marnie thinks she's laughing at *her*.

But Marnie hasn't noticed. She's pointing at Bee.

'What's up with *him*?' asks Marnie, spotting that Bee is shaking, his tail between his legs – spooked at the appearance and then disappearance of another dog, I suppose.

'He gets like that when he needs a run around,' I lie quickly. 'Is it OK if we let him out into the garden?'

'Yes, of course!' says Etta, blinking and smiling herself back into the conversation. 'Dear me . . . what were we talking about, girls? It's gone completely out of my mind, silly old woman that I am!'

Sweet, kind lady that you are, I think, as I take Bee by the collar and lead him towards the back door.

I totally get why Etta needs the angels' help now. Everyone can cope with bad stuff, but the problem is when it all collides together. *That's* when a person's shine starts to fade drastically.

For me, my best friend Tia emigrating made me

so, so lonely it brought out all the longing for Mum that I'd had locked away inside.

For Woody, everything came crashing down when he struggled with his dyslexia, plus the teasing that went with it, and he nearly got into terrible trouble at school.

For Etta, it's about losing her home and her husband and her beloved dog all in one harsh, hard-to-take blow.

But with the angels to gently guide her to happiness she'll be shining again soon. I know it, even if she doesn't.

'Oh, Riley – I just remembered!' Etta suddenly calls out after me. 'I think I might have something for you, something from your mum's shop.'

I stop dead. The florist's is now a children's shop, selling buggies and cots and stuff. I've been inside once, with Pearl. She did a telling on me, and I stood there smelling the mixed scents of the flowers, watching Mum serving someone. Mum,

who was pregnant with me, serving a customer called Etta . . .

'I'll have to dig it out for you – if you want it, that is? It's only a scrap of paper, but it might be a nice little memento?'

I turn and smile at Etta. 'Yes, please,' I say, feeling my *own* shine glow a little brighter . . .

Older, wiser, waggier

'Come on in, Riley!' says Mrs Angelo, waving me inside. 'Everything . . . all right?'

Oops. She's caught me standing staring at her.

It's just that sometimes I look at nice, ordinary Mrs Angelo and her husband and wonder what on earth they'd think if they knew their foster kids were really from . . . wherever they're from.

It's as if they've got three superheroes living in their loft, while they're downstairs watching telly or ordering their online groceries.

Weird.

'Fine, thanks,' I reply, after giving myself a shake

and remembering to act normal. I need to act like I'm here to talk about school gossip and funny YouTube clips with my friends, instead of grilling them about what strangeness happened at Marnie's house this afternoon.

'Good, good,' says Mrs Angelo, closing the front door behind me. 'We've just finished tea, and the girls have gone upstairs to do their homework.'

Bet they're not doing that, I think, smiling to myself and bounding up the stairs. The angels don't need to study for any schoolwork. Somehow, somewhere, they've been primed with all they need to know to fit in at school and pass as (almost) everyday students.

Two flights of stairs up, and I'm slightly out of breath and lifting my hand to *tap-tap* on the loft-room door.

'Hi,' says Kitt, opening it up before I've even started knocking. *She really is very good at catching*, I think, as I walk in, passing the skills chart on the wall. (For a second, I see it the way Mr and Mrs Angelo do, with the cutesy 'WELCOME TO OUR

126

HOME SWEET HOME!' message – then I blink and it's back to the chart dotted with ticks and crosses.)

'Hi,' I reply to Kitt, and wave at Sunshine and Pearl, who are sitting on the floor of this airy sky-blue and cloud-white room. You know, I always get a thrill walking in here; the loft now seems impossibly big, much, *much* bigger than it was when it was Tia's bedroom.

Together with Kitt, I flop down on to one of the fluffy white pillows piled on the white-painted floorboards. Even Bee is resting his shaggy head and paws on one.

Since the angels aren't really into small talk, as soon as I get settled, I ask the obvious question. 'So how did it happen? How did Alastair come to life? Who did the errant magic?'

'Bee!' Pearl answers brightly. Then her face falls when she realizes how much her sisters are suddenly frowning at her.

I'm doing the opposite of frowning. My eyebrows have shot halfway up my forehead, I'm sure.

Bee?

I am so surprised I can hardly breathe.

BEE?!

Shock has hit me hard in the chest, like I just did the worst bellyflop in the history of the local leisure centre swimming pool.

'Are you ill, Riley?' asks Pearl, tilting her head as she stares at me.

They're *all* staring at me. Pearl, Sunshine, Kitt – and Bee.

'Bee . . . can *do* that stuff?' I check. 'But he's a *dog*. How is that possible?'

Sunshine seems about to talk, possibly to spin me a line, and then she pauses, dropping her head.

The pause lasts for a long, long time.

And then, finally, she brushes her long waves of hair away from her face and tells me the truth. 'Because he's an angel too.'

She said that so matter-of-factly.

But Bee being an *angel*, it doesn't sound like something that's very matter-of-fact to me.

A whole silent minute has passed and I *still* can't take it in. I stare down at Bee, who pounds his tail happily on the floor.

'Bee felt so sorry for Etta that he just . . . slipped,' Pearl dips back into her explanation.

'All this time,' I say, still staring at their fluffy, fuzzy mound of dog, 'he's been a trainee angel, same as you?'

I guess it makes sense. Bee's always seemed way too smart for even the smartest of dogs. I mean, he walks with us to school every day, then takes himself off home, waiting patiently at the crossing on Meadow Lane till the green man comes on, and he can cross the dual carriageway safely. He scampers up and down the treehouse ladder without the slightest hesitation. And it's always seemed uncanny the way he tunes into everything that Sunshine, Kitt and Pearl say and do.

'Oh, he's not a trainee,' Kitt informs me, stroking Bee's head. 'He's our guide.'

Thump.

129

Another ripple of aftershock slams me hard in the chest.

'He's an older, wiser one,' Sunshine adds, trying to be helpful, though I still don't really understand.

Meanwhile, Bee – who's always had the doggy grin of a golden retriever – positively beams at me now, his tail drumming manically on the floorboards.

'If we get really stuck, he can give us advice,' says Pearl.

And then I remember times when Pearl has piped up, 'Should we ask for help?' and her sisters have shushed her. She was talking about Bee. Four-legged, fuzzy angel-in-charge Bee. Older, wiser, *waggier*.

How am I going to get my head round this?

And, hey, the other day in the treehouse, when I thought Pearl was saying someone else's words, they were his, weren't they? And when she 'accidentally' held Bee too tight . . . she was covering his ears so

he couldn't hear, wasn't she? So she wouldn't get into trouble for talking to me about things she shouldn't.

Tap-tap-tap.

Head-spinningly bizarre as this moment is, ordinary life has come knocking.

'Come in!' Sunshine calls out, and Mr Angelo's head pops round the door.

'Hi, girls! Can I grab a couple of you to help me get the washing in? I forgot it was out there, and the rain's just starting.'

Sunshine and Pearl jump to their feet and follow him straight away. Which leaves me and Kitt.

Earlier in the week, I'd hoped to get her on her own, and now here we are. Only we aren't quite as alone as I'd expected.

'So . . . can I talk to him?' I ask her.

'Not the way we can, no,' says Kitt. 'You can scratch his ears, though. He likes that.'

'But he's not a dog,' I say stupidly, cos my head has melted.

'Well, no.' Kitt laughs at my dopiness. 'Though we're not like *this* either, are we?' She points at her schoolgirl self.

'You mean –' I stumble, struggling with this new information – 'if I took a photo of him . . .'

'It would be the same as us,' says Kitt, beating me to it. 'Yes.'

Bee the dog would be a dancing twinkle of light, just as Sunshine, Kitt and Pearl are in the photo I took of them up at Folly Hill.

'Kitt . . .' I begin. It's the perfect point to ask about where the angels came from, but the problem is that my tongue – as well as my head – is in a knot.

'Wait. Let me see,' Kitt orders in her no-messing style, and leans over to stare into my eyes.

And so I relax. I pull some kind of mental curtain back and allow Kitt's darkening eyes to bore into my feeble, crashed brain. *Will she make any sense of what's in there?*

She blinks, and her eyes return to the grey-blue of the sky outside the loft windows.

Is she done?

Does she have an answer for me?

'You've seen them,' says Kitt, confusing me. 'Pearl showed you.'

No! What have I done? I fret, dropping my head into my hands.

When Kitt stared into my messed-up bedroom of a head just now, my question must have been hiding under some chucked-aside clothes on the floor.

Instead, Kitt's camera-sharp vision zoomed in on that moment a few weeks ago in Marnie's garden, the day of the party. Where delicately, with a shaking, nervous hand, Pearl had untied the small, so-soft, blue silk bundle and shown me her very own set of skills. Those tiny, trembling spheres with a texture like gel. I can still picture the way they'd quivered and shivered, bumped and jerkily spun.

Pearl shouldn't have shown me. She knew it was wrong; revealing this ultimate secret would be worse in her sisters' eyes than being discovered doing any amount of errant magic.

And now here I was, spilling my friend's deepest, brightest secret without meaning to . . . Kitt will be furious with her. Sunshine's calm face will tighten with anger. Bee will . . . I don't know what Bee will do. Growl?

A weight lands on my lap and I let my hands drop away.

Bee's head is on me and, same as any loving, lovable dog, he makes puppy eyes at us, as if he wants to cheer me up.

'Here,' says Kitt, who must have moved away while my eyes were shut, because she's shuffling back to me now. 'These are mine . . .'

Kitt pulls a thin metallic thread, and a blue silk bag opens up, falling away like delicate petals. And there, cupped in the centre of her palm, are nine shining, glowing, pulsating orbs. They roll around each other smoothly and freely, turning and tumbling.

Thud-thud, goes my heart, dazed.

Tell me more, goes my head, charmed.

'They're different from Pearl's,' I comment, hoping I'm not saying something out of turn, that I'm not marking Pearl down or something.

'I'm a little more advanced, remember,' Kitt says, gazing down at her skills with obvious pride. 'But Pearl's are better and brighter since you last saw them.'

I feel reassured. Pearl only showed them to me because she was worried, scared that the errant magic she'd done was damaging them.

'You can touch them if you like,' Kitt offers.

'Really?' I gasp, thrilled that she trusts me with her most precious –

Rat-a-tat! A banging comes from the loft door.

'Hi!' says Woody, grinning his way into the room before Kitt has a chance to invite him in. 'Hey, Kitt, your, er . . . I mean, Mr Angelo said I should come right up!'

Has Woody noticed what Kitt was holding? Is he

at all curious about the bundle she's now shoved under the nearest pillow on the floor?

'So . . . you guys OK?' he asks with a grin, hovering by the door and not sure what to do with himself. Woody might be a dork but he can definitely sense an atmosphere of some kind.

Kitt's face is clouded, I notice. Is she disappointed with herself? Catching is one of her best skills, but she was so busy showing me her own secret skill set that she didn't sense Woody's presence in the house, his Vans thumping up the stairs towards us.

'Um, yeah,' I reply, hoping I can act normal. Though that's a big ask, considering what I've found out and been shown in the last few minutes.

'I went round to your place a minute ago, Riley,' Woody chatters on, 'but your dad said you were here.'

'I am . . . here,' I say slightly uselessly, but that's because I can see Bee nuzzling an escaped skill back under the pillow with his nose.

'Well, I just wanted to catch up,' he carries on.

'I heard at school about what you guys did in your music lesson today. Heard it was pretty awesome.'

He's directing his words to Kitt, and I can see him gazing around, wondering where her sisters are, since they're nearly always together.

'It *was* pretty awesome,' I tell him, as Kitt has temporarily forgotten that human conversation needs people to respond to each other.

'Well, hey, I was thinking,' Woody carries on. 'We should do an interview for *News Matters*, with Sunshine and Pearl too?'

He's holding up his phone, since that's what he plans to record the interview on.

He has no idea that two of his interviewees are standing silently behind him in the doorway.

He is grinning in his dorky, hopeful way, unaware that Sunshine, Kitt and Pearl are communicating an urgent thought to each other.

My friends are trying to work out what he saw, *if* he saw, and whether or not they need to rewind him.

But a rewind is tough. The hardest of the skills, it's tiring and draining to take people back, even just to return them in time by a few minutes. If the angels don't need to, they shouldn't.

And I might be a skill-free, semi-useless non-angel, but I *can* read body language. And Woody's relaxed, dorky-as-usual body language is telling me that he saw nothing he shouldn't have.

How do I let the angels know that?

Sunshine and Pearl's eyes are twinkling behind him, as they get ready to make the magic happen.

I bite my lip, then feel myself frantically humming the four notes of the earworm tune that's been coming to me this week.

Something about humming them fast seems to clear my mind.

All I need is to shout one word.

DON'T, I yell with all my might, but in the privacy of my head.

It's worked! They heard . . .

Sunshine and Pearl, Kitt and Bee. They all turn

to stare at me – but their eyes are returning to normal, the brightness fading.

'So, what do you think?' Woody asks, scratching casually at his freckly nose.

I smile to myself. *I think you have no idea what nearly happened to you . . .*

The face in the photo

It's Friday. We're in a *News Matters* meeting. And I'm saying yes to something I can't possibly do.

'So, we'll need a photo of Sunshine, Kitt and Pearl to go with their interview,' Daniel is saying. 'You OK to sort that out, Riley?'

'Yes,' I lie.

Of course I can't take a photo of them. I can't exactly download an image of three dots of light and tell the team it's the best I can do.

But, hey, I'm not worrying about my lie. I plan on taking so many good photos at the Frost Fair tomorrow that Daniel and the rest of the school-newsletter team will forget all about a picture to go with the girls' interview. (It helps that Marnie is planning to wear a green-velvet medieval-style dress that our drama teacher found left over from a Shakespeare production.)

'And you two are all set to cover the fair tomorrow?' Hannah checks with me and Woody. She has a pad in front of her, a pencil scritch-scratching notes of our meeting.

'Yep, me and Riley are set,' says Woody, answering for us both. '*And* I've got a whole load of background information. I even found out that people tried to revive the Frost Fair about ten years ago, but it never happened.'

Woody pulls out photocopied pages from old editions of the local paper. He's been busy.

'Yeah, well, that's all sounding pretty organized,' says Mr Edwards. 'But I think you still need something *else* in this issue. Anyone got any other ideas? Maybe something to do with resolutions, since it's the first newsletter of the year?'

There's silence for a moment as we all think.

We jump when Ceyda coughs, expecting some fab suggestion, but turns out it was just a cough.

'Hey, *I* know!'

We all jump again at Woody's short, sharp exclamation.

'Riley's little sister came up with this kind of cool idea the other day.'

I don't correct Woody (it takes too long to say she's my little sort-of-stepsister cos Dad and Hazel aren't married). Also, I'm curious to find out what he's on about.

'We were up on Folly Hill on Monday, weren't we, Riley?' Woody begins to explain.

Wow, Monday seems like forever ago now. This week's been such an up-high, down-low, twisty-turny roller-coaster of a ride so far.

Woody takes my nod for agreement and carries on.

'Now Dot's only five, right? And she asks us this pretty funny question. She obviously doesn't know what a resolution is, so she asked us what our New Year *Wish* would be. So how about we do a vox pop around school? Find out what people's New Year Wishes are?'

'Bet we'd get some pretty random answers!' says Billy, grinning.

'We could ask teachers and staff as well as students,' Daniel adds enthusiastically.

And they're all off, a chattering huddle of suggestions and ideas.

Which leaves me to sit back and drift off for a moment, lost in a snapshot memory of Folly Hill on Monday, wind whipping, clouds dashing.

Of course, none of my random three New Year's Wishes could be used in the *News Matters* feature.

I can't exactly shout to the world that my friends are angels.

That I'm so proud and happy that they like me enough to be my friend.

Or that I'd love to feel close to my mum . . .

Well, I guess they could print that last one, but it

might sound as if I'm feeling horribly sorry for myself. Then again, people could end up feeling horribly sorry *for* me, and I'd have to hear 'Do you know what happened to Riley's mum?' whispers in the playground.

So yeah, I'd better put that particular wish out of my mind.

Same as the angels seem to have put Mum out of *their* minds. Pearl/Bee said I'd find out more about her 'soon', but just how long is 'soon'? The girls have been so wrapped up in important stuff like seeking and searching and sharpening their skills that soon seems very far away from where I'm standing . . .

And then my eyes dip down to the scatter of pages Woody has spread out on the desk.

Black type on white paper.

Columns of words, blocks of headlines.

Photos of the lake, with its halo of tangled shrubs around it.

Photos of someone smiling.

Someone smiling out at me.

Someone I know better than anyone, though I don't really know her at all . . .

Brrrrüünggggg!

As the bell jangles everyone into action, chairs are scraped back, bags are grabbed and the pieces of paper are scooped up in Woody's hands.

'Please – can I see those?' I ask Woody urgently, once we're out of the classroom and in the stream of students in the corridor.

'Uh, sure . . . why?' Woody asks, handing me the untidy bundle of A4 sheets.

My hands are shaking as I take them and shuffle through them, trying to find her again.

'Here,' I say, as her face appears. 'This . . . this is my mum.'

'Yeah? Wow – so your mum was leading the Frost Fair campaign back then,' says Woody, tapping on the paper. 'You never told me!'

'I didn't know,' I say, stunned and surprised as I scan the article.

But there she is, talking. Or as close to talking

as I can get. Those quote marks round Mum's words make her feel almost alive to me as I read them aloud.

'"*Organized by Lord Hillcrest and his daughter Grace, the Frost Fair of* 1814 *was a fantastic community event*," says Annie Roberts. "*It could be a fantastic community event again, even if it is on dry land this time! And if we could work towards restoring Lady Grace's Lake to its former beauty, that would be wonderful too.*"'

'Well, you'd better have this, then,' Woody tells me. He doesn't ask any more, probably because I don't really talk about Mum. I mean, he's seen her photo on my bedside table, and knows she died when I was a baby, but that's it.

Still, all of a sudden I find myself looking at him, wondering if I'm acting too much like Dad, if I should open up and tell my friend how much I miss my –

'Hey, Riley,' I hear a familiar voice call out to me.

It's Marnie, wending her way towards us through

the crush of students. From the intense way she's looking at me, I don't need to be psychic to guess she has something to tell me.

OK, make that *show* me, since she's waving something in her hand.

'Here – Nan managed to find this for you,' says Marnie, reaching out and passing me a little slip of card. 'It's something from your mum's shop.'

I take the card from her. It's small and rectangular, with a little posy of flowers printed on it (printed by Dad, obviously). There's pretty, slopey handwriting to the right of the posy.

With all my love, always, sweetheart . . . it says.

I have a fluttering feeling in my chest, wondering if I'm right, if this is what I think it is.

'Grandad sent Nan a bunch of flowers one time, and this was the gift card that was with it,' Marnie explains. 'Nan kept it in a box of letters and stuff. Anyway, she told me to tell you that Grandad ordered the bouquet from your mum's shop and so –'

'And so this is my mum's handwriting . . .' I finish off, hardly believing my luck.

A minute ago, I got the gift of her face, smiling up at me.

Then another gift, reading her words.

And now I have this simple slip of white card that connects me directly to my mother. She picked this up with her fingers, same as I'm doing now. Her hand held a pen and wrote these words that my fingers are now running over, feeling the indent of the letters on the card. And the message.

I know it was a loving message from Marnie's grandfather to his wife, but this very second it's as if my mum's whispering those same words to me, a murmur of love through the years . . .

'You OK?' says Woody.

'Yeah,' I say softly, feeling more than OK. I feel amazing. Like my New Year Wish to get closer to Mum is actually coming true.

'Look – me and Marnie better go. Our next class

is over in the other block and we'll be late if we don't head there now.'

'Sure.' I look up at him and Marnie, smiling my thanks at her.

I feel suddenly floaty light, as if a weight has been lifted off my shoulders. If I want to – and I think I might want to – I can talk about Mum with these two friends. It's as if she doesn't have to be my guilty secret any more.

'Catch up later, yeah?' says Woody, giving me a playful soft punch on the arm.

As he and Marnie go one way, another friend drifts reassuringly towards me.

Sunshine is peeling away from a conversation that's been happening further up the corridor, leaving Kitt and Pearl talking to Mr Hamdi.

'You look happy,' she says to me.

'No purple?' I joke, wafting my hand around my head. I'm stress-free, which is a nice thing to be.

'No purple.' Sunshine smiles. 'What's that?'

I show her the card, then I hold out the sheet I've

been clutching in my other hand. Sunshine's violet-blue eyes forensically scan everything put in front of them.

'It's like . . . like I've been given a little bit of her,' I tell my friend, struggling to put my happiness into words she might understand.

Sunshine tilts her head a little, letting her wavy red waves tumble away from her shoulder. 'Mothers never leave you, even when they're gone,' she says simply.

And I want to burst with the love I have for this strange and wonderful girl standing in front of me.

Only she's not really a girl, is she?

'Sunshine?' I say in a voice only she can hear, mouthing quiet words at her. 'What exactly are –'

Before I get a chance to ask her the question I asked her sisters, she turns and goes, leaving me with one thing.

It's a word.

'Soon . . .'

The spring and the secrets

Downstairs the TV is blaring with some movie that Dot is glued to. (I hear her warbling about snow, so I reckon it's *Frozen*.)

There's a distant clatter of pots and pans as Dad gets the tea ready. (Hazel will be home from her shift at the hospital soon.)

I'm sitting on my bedroom floor with Sunshine, Kitt and Pearl. (Bee is spread out beside us, unnerving me slightly now I know what he is – and what he isn't.)

In the middle of our circle of girls, three things are laid out: the handwritten gift card Etta gave me, the photocopy of the newspaper feature from Woody, and Mum's framed photo.

'Are you sure this will work?' I ask them. They've done tellings before, but not like this.

'No,' says Kitt, blunt as ever.

'But Bee says it might!' Pearl adds hopefully.

I look over at Bee, who pants and wags his tail. It's going to take a while to get my head round a fluffy, scruffy white dog being 'in charge'.

'I know we usually do this on living people, but let's try . . .'

Sunshine holds out a hand to me, and places the other one down flat on the news article. Following her lead, Pearl places a finger on the Annie's Posies card, while Kitt rests her hand on the frame of Mum's photo.

I take a deep breath, and watch as the angels' eyes begin to brighten and glow.

After rewind, telling is the second-strongest skill. When Pearl did it to me, I could smell the flowers in Mum's shop, hear her chatting to a customer

(Marnie's nan, as it turned out), and see Mum moving around, alive and well and with a baby bump that was me.

I guess you could say that a telling is a wonderful window into your life, a 3-D snapshot of a time or place or person.

But Mum isn't a living, breathing person any more. Do the angels have enough power to conjure up a memory from Mum's past from these scraps of paper, however special they are to me?

I feel the flutter and warmth of vibration in the hand that's holding Sunshine's. Their energy is rising, their eyes are silvering.

'Please work . . .' I mutter softly to myself. 'Please work . . .'

Even with my pleading words, it's no good.

The angels try their hardest but almost as soon as it's begun, I feel the vibration fading.

A soft warm face lands in my lap. I look down into Bee's puppy-dog eyes, and sigh.

'Sorry,' says Sunshine.

'It's OK,' I reply. But I could cry with disappointment.

Today felt so special, so important. The coincidence of seeing Mum in the Frost Fair article and *then* seeing her writing on the gift card . . . Maybe it was dumb, but it made me feel like it wouldn't stop there.

These were signs that some amazing break-through was just round the corner.

Something to do with Mum that would blow my mind . . .

But that's not going to happen, is it?

A huge full stop just went splat in my heart.

If only –

Tappity-tap!

'Can I come in?'

Wow. Maybe it's just as well the telling didn't work. Same as usual, Dad smiles his way round my door before I've properly answered him.

What on earth would he have made of my friends in a trance, with slivers of light beaming from them?

'Dot demanded lemonade, so I thought I'd bring you girls some up too,' says Dad, joggling his way in, carrying a tray with tall glasses. 'Hey, do you know what I caught her doing? Dancing around to the film wearing Hazel's favourite bra on top of her jumper. She says it's all lacy and pretty, just like a princess would wear!'

'She's definitely into helping herself to stuff at the moment.' I'm careful not to use the word 'steal' since that didn't go down too well the last time I said it.

'Let's call it a "magpie" phase,' Dad suggests, grinning. 'It's quite common in kids her age, apparently, though thankfully you weren't like that, Riley! Well, not that I can remem–'

Dad pauses. His gaze has dropped to the floor, and now he's slumped quickly down on to his knees. The tray lands awkwardly, and the lemonade slops out of the glasses.

'Where did you get this?' Dad asks me, reaching out to pick up the news article.

155

Sunshine, Kitt and Pearl stare passively at Dad. They're studying him, his tightened jaw and his whitened face, as if he was an interesting science experiment.

'Woody found it in an old local paper. It's for the piece we're doing on the Frost Fair for the school newsletter,' I explain, watching his reaction closely. The last time I mentioned the Frost Fair, Dad went quiet and stomped off.

This time he's busy staring, with no sign of stomping. So I risk saying something about her . . .

'I didn't know Mum was into campaigning.'

Of course, I don't know lots about Mum, since Dad virtually never talks about her.

'Annie knew so much about the history of Hillcrest Manor and the whole area,' he says softly, staring into Mum's face. 'She loved Folly Hill, and the lake too. She wanted it to be returned to the way it looked originally. There was a lot of support for her idea to fundraise and hold the Frost Fair. But then . . .'

No! He's doing what he *always* does: going silent on me.

OK, so my dad may not be talking but there is one word I can clearly hear.

A word that's being whispered in my mind.

'*Spring*,' Sunshine is telling her sisters.

And, before Dad knows it, he's babbling, chattering, as if he has no control of his mouth, his words.

'The girl . . . she was only a teenager, lost in her music . . .'

He pauses for a second, picturing someone. I'm just not sure *who* he's picturing.

'Annie saw her step out. Not looking. As if Meadow Lane was nothing . . . The lorry driver . . . he thought he'd hit the girl . . .'

Mum's accident.

The memory hurts so much Dad's almost grinding his teeth. Part of me wants the angels to stop the spring, but part of me needs to know everything. Even if it's the saddest thing I've ever heard.

'People thought the scream . . . that it meant the girl was hurt, but it was the shock of Annie shoving her so hard . . . Annie was brave, so, so brave.'

I didn't know about the daydreaming teenage girl, but I know Mum died that day, that second. The lorry must've hit her just after she'd pushed the girl out of the way.

'I am so, SO angry with Annie!' Dad suddenly explodes, his face reddening. 'I lost her and . . . and . . .'

This isn't good. This is too much, I think, my chest heaving with panic.

Sensing my stress, or Dad's, Bee begins to whimper, alerting the angels. Almost instantly, Sunshine lifts her hand to Dad's head, letting the warmth soothe him.

'My baby girl and me . . . So angry . . . Annie shouldn't have left us . . .'

Dad's shoulders are sinking, as if he wants to collapse into the ground, worn down with the unfairness of it all.

I shuffle over and give him a cuddle, even though he's unaware of what I'm doing. And then I feel the change, the release.

Sunshine lifts her hand from Dad's head and sits back beside Kitt and Pearl.

The angels – their eyes now different shades of blue that could *almost* pass for normal – gaze peacefully at me and Dad.

'Hey, I – um –' Dad stumbles around with his words, a little dizzy and confused. He has no idea what just happened and is probably wondering why I'm snuggled into him.

I guess I *could* take advantage of our sudden close contact and talk to him more about the newspaper picture or the Frost Fair. But Dad looks so frazzled and tired that I forget it – and kiss him on the cheek instead.

'Ha!' he laughs. 'Kissing your dad in front of your cool friends? What did I do to deserve that?'

'They don't mind and I don't care,' I tell him. 'And you deserve it because I love you.'

Dad looks straight into my eyes for a split-second, as though he's weighing something up. Deciding whether or not to tell me something, I'm sure. And then he speaks.

'I love you too, honey. And there's something you deserve to have. Here, come with me,' he says, holding a hand out to me.

As we get to our feet and go towards the door, I glance back at the angels. All four of them, including Bee, smile a knowing smile. Is this a catch? Do they know what's about to happen?

'After your mum died,' Dad is saying, as he leads the way through to his and Hazel's bedroom, 'I didn't keep many of her things. It was too hard to have reminders. So I gave it all away, except for those few photos –'

Which I now have, I think to myself, while Dad bends and opens the door of his bedside cabinet.

'And this one thing she loved. It's only a bag full of silly trinkets. But for some reason they were very special to her.'

Dad rummages around in the cabinet, pushing aside books and assorted bits and bobs. His searching starts carefully – but then becomes more frantic.

'Where are they?' he says urgently. 'I *never* move them. They're always at the back here!'

'What are you doing?' comes a small shy voice.

Dad and I swing our heads round and see Dot in the doorway, clutching Alastair, as usual. In her outfit of tutu, jumper, stolen lacy bra and tiara, she looks adorably silly and cute. But, to me, she also looks *guilty*.

'Dot, have you taken anything from here, maybe to play with?' Dad asks in as calm a voice as he can manage. He's obviously spotted the guilty look too.

'No!' Dot replies, with pinkening cheeks. 'Well, only some marbles. I didn't think you'd mind, Stuart, cos marbles are really a CHILDREN'S toy, not for grown-ups!'

I'm only half listening to her excuse.

I'm suddenly icy cold, as chilled to the bone as if I was in a scene from *Frozen*.

'Go and get them at once!' Dad orders Dot, sounding more annoyed than I've ever heard him.

Dot looks like she might cry.

And I think *I* might cry.

Mum, my mum, had her own set of skills?

Which means Annie Roberts – wife, mum, florist, tragic heroine – was an *angel*?

With a scream and a splash

Magical mixed with spooky crossed with pretty.

That's how fairground music has always sounded to me. And today, considering what I've been through, it makes the perfect soundtrack.

That and the words Sunshine, Kitt and Pearl whispered in my head yesterday evening, when they appeared in Dad's bedroom doorway. Though Dad and Dot heard nothing, each girl repeated a phrase over and over, like a meditation to calm my exploding head.

'It's true . . . true . . . true . . .'

'Be patient . . . be patient . . . be patient . . .'

'*It will all make sense . . . it will all make sense . . . it will all make sense . . .*'

So here I am at the Frost Fair, still trying to let the truth sink in, being patient, and wondering if I can *ever* make sense of what I've found out about Mum.

And, while my mind whirls, girls and boys slide and screech their way down the helter-skelter. Horses on poles prance up and down on their ornately painted roundabout. Fathers impatiently wait their turn as children throw balls at coconuts and miss every time.

I stop and snap, capturing colourful moments on my camera, while Woody records his thoughts into his phone.

'This newly cleared patch of land around the lake has been transformed into a winter wonderland,' he is muttering. 'For generations this special spot has been overgrown and almost abandoned. But today marks the start of an amazing transformation – for the first time in decades, the Angel on Folly Hill can gaze down from on high and catch a glimpse of the lake she once looked out over.'

'Why is Woody talking to himself?' Pearl asks me, sounding a lot like Dot, who also happens to be around here somewhere, with Dad, Hazel and Coco.

'It's cos of his dyslexia,' Marnie explains, holding her long green-velvet dress up so she doesn't trip over. 'It's much easier for Woody to record stuff than write it down.'

'Oh *yes*!' says Pearl, sounding delighted, which is obviously the wrong response.

Marnie frowns at Pearl, mistaking her goofiness for rudeness. She has no idea that Pearl and her sisters worked very hard to restore Woody's shine. But then, apart from me, nobody does, including Woody.

'Look – I think that Mr Hamdi is waving to us,' Kitt suddenly points out, perhaps covering up for her sister.

I glance up from my camera and see that Kitt's right – Mr Hamdi is waving everyone over towards

the main marquee. It must be time for the concert to start.

'Are you all right?' Sunshine asks me with quiet words, as we all move through the crowds towards the tent.

'Yes,' I say out loud, very sure of my answer.

I'm in shock still, of course. And shocked that I'm managing to act vaguely normal.

In fact, I acted normal when Dad handed me the rescued silky blue bundle of 'marbles' yesterday (if only he knew what they *were*).

I acted normal after the angels left to go home for their tea (my mind was as tangled as the spaghetti on my plate).

I acted normal when I went to bed (then lay awake, trying to absorb this bolt from the blue, the amazing wonder of it all).

I acted normal when I headed off with my friends to the lake today (though I slipped the bundle of dull dark spheres into my bag, alongside my camera).

My fingers slide into my canvas bag now, searching for the coolness of the silk under my fingers.

'You will explain everything to me soon, won't you?' I ask Sunshine.

Of all the astounding surprises that have happened since the angels arrived, finding out Mum was an angel is the most staggering, astonishing and life-changing.

'Riley, you must be patient,' Sunshine repeats to me now, linking her arm in mine. 'It will –'

'All make sense,' I finish for her, giving in to the fact that Sunshine isn't about to pull me into the fortune-teller's booth and show me my past, present and future in a crystal ball.

'Hurry, people!' says Mr Hamdi, ushering us all inside the marquee. 'The audience is ready and waiting! Are you OK to go first, Marnie?'

Marnie nods and takes the flute Mr Hamdi's been looking after for her. Hoisting up her beautiful but lethally long dress, she lets Woody help her up on to the stage.

There are rumbles of *ooh*s when the audience sees how authentically she's dressed, and how totally elegant she looks too, with her black bob scraped back into a tight, low bun.

As the haunting strains of 'Greensleeves' drift out, I move around, taking photos from different angles. In between shots, I glance at the crowd, seeing lots of friendly but unfamiliar faces, as well as students and a couple of teachers I recognize from school. Mr and Mrs Angelo are near the back, sipping what looks like mulled wine. No sign of Dad, Hazel, Dot and Coco, though.

I hope they don't miss the angels; they're due to sing next.

Then I spot a couple of people I'm really, really pleased to see. Marnie's nan Etta, and her mum too. They don't seem to be warring for once, which will make a nice change for Marnie.

'We left some warmth hidden in their kitchen,' Kitt whispers in quiet words, obviously spotting who I'm looking at. 'Bee told us it will last a while.

But we need to find a way to be closer to Etta, so we can work out how to help find her shine.'

I want to ask how and where they hid the warmth, but my head is so full of strangeness that it's the least of my worries.

'Thank you very much, Marnie Reynolds! Fabulous!' Mr Hamdi says into the microphone over the barrage of applause. 'And next we have three girls with the most *angelic* voices. I give you Sunshine, Kitt and Pearl Angelo!'

There's a smattering of clapping, a roar from the back (their foster father, Frank Angelo, maybe?) and – very annoyingly – a snigger or two.

I think the sniggering is because the angels haven't dressed in costume. It wouldn't occur to them to do that, I suppose. They see no problem in singing an ancient choral song wearing colourful winter duffel jackets and wellie boots.

Or, of course, it could be the fact that the audience has seen a dog trotting on stage with them and making itself comfortable next to the monitors.

But, as soon as they open their mouths, the perfect, pure notes of 'Gaudete' soar as high as the roof of the tent, and gasps of awe ripple all around me.

For the few minutes the short piece lasts, it's as if everyone is holding their breath at the beauty of it. When the song ends, the applause is as loud as a hundred balloons bursting.

Sunshine, Kitt and Pearl glance at each other and exchange small, pleased smiles.

Mr Hamdi walks forward to the microphone to thank them. But he's stopped in his tracks. The girls have launched into another song. And the first four notes grab my attention straight away, the hairs on my arms instantly prickling and tickling.

'*Lavender's blue . . .*' the girls sing.

'*. . . dilly, dilly,*' I join in softly, finally realizing what the tune is that I've been hearing snatches of all week.

'*Lavender's green . . .*'

I hum along to the song, while people all

around me hum and mutter too, wondering why the oddly cool girls on stage have chosen to sing such an old-fashioned nursery rhyme.

It's when they come to one line that I suddenly understand why.

'*If you love me, dilly dilly, I will love you . . .*'

Mum.

It was the song she always sang to me as a baby. Holding me close, rocking me gently, words soft and warm around me, then a kiss – always a kiss – on my forehead when she came to that line.

Mum.

My New Year Wish was to feel closer to her, and everything that happened this week, everything I've discovered, has been incredible. But this moment, this memory that the angels have given me, is the best gift ever. With that song, it's as if her arms are round me, holding me like she'll never let me go . . .

'Well! Fantastic choice, girls!' Mr Hamdi says into the microphone. 'I suppose that nowadays people might think of that as a simple nursery

rhyme, but it is in fact a traditional folk song that dates back centuries.'

There are some *aah*s around me as people make sense of the girls' song choice.

Oh, and one *boo* . . . followed by giggles.

Along with everyone else, I scan the crowd to see who booed. What stupid, mean idiot would ruin the moment – my moment – like that?

Then I spot her blonde hair, her sniggering friends. Of course, who else would it be?

I feel a rage building inside me . . .

'All right, ladies and gentlemen, boys and girls,' says Mr Hamdi, holding a piece of paper up in front of him. 'I've been told to let you know that the stocks are now open.'

Sunshine, Kitt and Pearl are getting down from the stage just as two men dressed as jesters jump up beside Mr Hamdi. At the mention of the stocks, they stick their thumbs in the air.

'So,' Mr Hamdi continues, 'if anyone fancies volunteering to get locked in the stocks and pelted

with wet sponges, put your hand up now. Anyone up for it? Anyone? Ah, a student from my own school! Well done, Lauren!'

Lauren Mayhew *offered* to go in the stocks? I watch in surprise as the two jesters jump off the stage and run over to her. Sure enough, Lauren's arm is held high above her. In a matter of seconds she's being cheerfully jostled out of the tent by the jesters, her arm still in the air but a look of panic on her face.

'No! I don't – I mean, I can't –'

A smile spreads across my face as I realize Lauren has no control of what her arm is doing. I'm seeing some errant magic going on, aren't I?

And whichever of my friends is responsible for it I'm going to have to thank them big time.

I glance over to look for them now – but instantly I sense trouble.

They're marooned at the edge of the stage, the crowd too closely packed for them to get over to me easily. But it's Kitt – with her talent for

catching – that is alerting me to something. Even from here I can see how intensely dark her eyes are.

'*Dot!*' Kitt's voice rings inside my head with a sense of urgency.

It's all I need. I spin round, frantically looking for signs of my little sort-of-stepsister. Instead I see Dad and Hazel at the entrance to the marquee quickly, desperately scanning the room.

'Excuse me, s'cuse me,' I mumble, squeezing myself through the crush to reach them.

As I get close, I see real fear in Hazel's eyes. And now Woody is by their side and Dad is telling him something.

'What?' I ask, finally forcing my way to them.

'Dot and Coco are missing,' says Hazel, ashen-faced and trembling.

'We were chatting to one of my clients from the shop, and the girls were a bit bored,' Dad explains at breakneck speed, 'so I gave them money for the hook-a-duck stall . . . but when we went to it just a couple of minutes later there was no sign of them!'

'Me and my friends can look for them too,' I say, looking to Woody to help me. But he's helping already, bless him.

'Marnie, I'm over by the entrance,' he's saying into his mobile, while waving at the stage, where Marnie's been chatting to Mr Hamdi. 'Bit of an emergency – Riley's kid sister and her friend are missing. Can you get on the mic and make an announcement?'

Everything happens in a rushed, fuzzy blur. As Marnie's voice booms out over the shuffling audience, the angels manage to join us and Dad suggests different areas for us all to check. We instantly fan out, and I'm running, running away from the fair towards the tangle of shrubs and the dog-walkers' path.

'Dot! Dot!' I call out, my chest heaving. 'Coco!'

Something brushes past my legs. Something soft and warm.

It's Bee and, knowing what I know about him, I'm happy he's with me.

I'm especially happy to have him when I see the path split into two up ahead, and I follow Bee as he confidently bounds down the right-hand fork.

I hurtle after him, aware that the sounds of the fair behind me are muffled by the dense shrubs all around.

'Dot! Coco!' I call again, hoping I'll be able to hear any response over the deafening thunder of my heart and the pounding of the pulse in my head.

But Bee's sudden barking is loud enough to grab my attention.

'DOT!' I yell louder, absolutely sure that the four-legged angel is leading me to her.

'Riley!' comes a thin, reedy voice that doesn't belong to my sister.

'Coco?' I call back, just as I stumble into a clearing by the lake's edge.

Bee barks up at a gnarly, knotty old tree with branches arcing over the water.

'Riley! We were climbing!' Coco squeaks, clinging

like a frightened bush baby to the twisted trunk of the tree. 'We can't get down. And Dot can't hold on!'

I glance further along the bent branches, and I suddenly spot Dot's blue coat.

'Dot – are you OK?' I shout, taking a few steps to one side to try to see her better.

She doesn't reply, which worries me madly. Dot is *never* quiet.

'HELP! Riley, I'm slipp–'

With a scream and a splash, she's disappearing below the surface, swallowed by the water.

Instantly I throw down my mobile and my bag, kick off my boots and desperately wriggle my heavy jacket off.

With nothing to weigh him down, Bee's in the water before me. And as I follow, wading and sloshing into the freezing lake, I fight back the fear that I'm not going to make it, that I'm not a good enough swimmer, that I won't have the strength to dive down and get her.

Every muscle in my back already aches with the effort.

'Please, please, please,' I murmur desperately, thigh-deep in muddy water now.

And then – just as I go to push off and swim – I catch sight of my reflection in the dark surface.

In that split-second I see something so shocking it makes me gasp, as if all the air in my lungs has been violently sucked out.

Because behind me, rising, are two wings.

I can hear the crackle and the rustle of them as they quiver higher.

I can feel the weight of them between my shoulder-blades.

And in that same split-second I hear a voice.

'*It'll be all right, Riley* . . .' Mum calls to me from the past.

Strength floods through me like a white heat and I dive in, ready to rescue my sister . . .

From Mum to me . . .

It's quite weird seeing a girl in medieval costume using a mobile phone.

'Come on, come on,' Marnie is muttering impatiently, as she stands at the entrance to the first-aid tent.

She's trying to get through to Dad, to let him know Dot and Coco have been found.

Woody's run off to ask for another announcement to be made, and hopefully to run into Dad and Hazel too.

I'm perched on a kind of camp bed, and have

just told the female first-aider that I'm fine sitting and that I don't want to lie down.

'Fair enough. Well, here,' she says, wrapping a crinkly silver blanket round me. 'This'll help warm you up.'

With relief, I realize she put it round me without gasping, without screaming at the sight of my wings.

Were they really ever there?

Was it just something I imagined to give me the strength to save Dot?

'Better?' I hear Etta asking.

She's sitting on a nearby folding chair, with my little sister on her lap. The older lady gently tucks Dot's own silver blanket more snuggly round her, while Coco, eyes wide, nibbles on a biscuit she's been given by the male first-aider.

Thank goodness for Etta.

She heard Marnie's first 'lost' alert, then spotted me and Bee run off.

It was just as well she decided to follow us . . . Etta had the steadiness to talk Coco down from the tree, and the sense to pick up all of our belongings – including my bag with Mum's set of skills in it, and Alastair, of course – as I carried Dot out of the water and to the safety of the first-aiders.

'Mmm.' Dot snuffles a reply to Etta's question, knuckles white as she clings on to Alastair. Is she worried that she might fall again if she doesn't hold on tight?

'And what about you, Riley, dear?' Etta asks, turning her attention to me. 'How are you feeling? You were awfully brave.'

As if he agrees, Bee licks my hand. Or maybe he's letting me know that I *didn't* imagine the wings . . .

'I'm just glad everything's OK,' I reply with a little shrug.

It's almost funny, describing 'everything' as 'OK'.

I need grand, sweeping words like 'staggering', 'overwhelming' and 'transforming'. But, if I come out with those right now, I worry the first-aiders might think I was delirious.

'Oh, look, Riley – here come your lovely friends!' Etta exclaims.

If I had a tail like Bee, I'd be wagging it same as him right now.

Although I'd like Dad and Hazel to be here with me, I need Sunshine, Kitt and Pearl even more, to help me make sense of my practically unrecognizable life.

'Now, not too much chatting all at once, girls!' says the male first-aider, spotting the girls heading over towards me. 'Your friend here has had a bit of a shock and we need to keep her calm.'

I certainly *have* had a shock, but not necessarily the one he is thinking of. And Sunshine, Kitt and Pearl are the perfect people to help calm me down.

Sunshine and Kitt sit themselves on either side of me, and Pearl pulls up another folding chair.

Placing her hand gently on my back, Sunshine simply says, 'Yes.'

'I have *wings*?' I check with her, although she's already answered my question.

'You're part angel because of your mother,' Sunshine says gently, while knocking me sideways with this information.

'You won't have all the skills in their full strength,' Kitt explains some more. 'But they will work well enough for you to help others.'

'Oh, and because you're not a pure angel, Riley, you don't actually have *physical* wings,' Pearl adds apologetically. 'But just sometimes, when you're alone, you might see them in a reflection.'

'I . . . I'll have powers?' I ask, still not taking it all in.

'Riley, you already have them,' says Sunshine.

'I *do*? How?'

Before anyone can reply, the male first-aider calls over to us. Oh no, in all the excitement, have we been talking way too loud? My heart lurches at the idea of our conversation being overheard.

'Hey, I know I said not to chat too much, but you girls don't have to be totally *silent*, you know!' he teases.

I stare stupidly at him, then feel a wave of relief . . . our conversation has been spoken entirely in quiet words, without me realizing. *There's* a power, a skill I have, for a start.

'You saw a purple haze in Marnie's kitchen,' Sunshine continues once the first-aider has turned his attention to someone who's walked in with a nosebleed. 'When her mother and grandmother were arguing, remember?'

'Yes! But I thought it was just the lighting!'

'And when we sang in class . . . when we opened up to the music, you held us tight, making sure we didn't lose ourselves too much.'

I rack my brain, trying to understand what Sunshine means, and then I get it; she's talking about singing along to 'Gaudete' in the music lesson. I was so worried about a repeat of Pearl nearly unfurling that I'd concentrated hard, barely breathing. I'd willed the angels to be all right, and it had worked. That's why Sunshine had whispered her thanks as we'd left the room.

'Of course, you will need to stop doing the errant magic, Riley . . .' Sunshine says now with a knowing smile playing at her lips.

'What do you mean?' I ask, blushing and flustered at the idea of doing something wrong without knowing what it was.

Pearl grins, Kitt snorts and even Sunshine giggles a little.

'*What?*' I demand.

'The gum in Lauren's hair on Tuesday? The fact that she ended up in the stocks today, because you forced her hand up?' says Kitt.

I slap my hands over my mouth to cover my surprise. Lauren's the mean girl around here – I don't want to be just as mean in return.

'I'm sorry . . . I can't believe I did that,' I mumble red-faced. 'It's so bad! I promise I won't do it again.'

'Well, you probably will, but learning not to takes practice,' Sunshine reassures me. 'And these –' Sunshine takes the blue silky bundle that Pearl's

holding out to her, the one she must've found in my bag just now – 'these will let you know when you're doing things right, and when you're doing them wrong.'

She places the bundle in my hand, but doesn't pull the silvery thread.

'There are too many people around to take them out,' Kitt explains. 'But you can feel them, can't you?'

I can!

I can feel the movement of the tiny spheres, delicately bumping and juddering and spinning in my palm!

'They were your mother's, but Bee helped us reignite them,' says Sunshine. 'They're yours now.'

So these skills are passing from Mum to *me*.

'Are you pleased, Riley?' Pearl asks excitedly, and out loud.

Pleased? It's too small a word again. I need to think up far more grand ones like . . . like . . .

'Riley!' I suddenly hear Dad call out.

'Dotty! Dotty, darling!' Hazel practically cries with relief.

'MUMMY!' Dot yelps, finding her big voice again, I'm pleased to hear.

I don't know whether Marnie got through to Dad on my phone, or if Woody's announcement alerted both of them to get here, but, whatever, I am *very* glad to see them.

'Woody told us what happened,' says Hazel, pausing beside me.

Uh-oh. My stomach lurches – what's she going to say? She hasn't exactly been impressed with me lately.

But, before I know what's happening, Hazel's scooping me up in a sudden hug.

'Thank you, *thank you*, Riley, for being the best big sister Dot could ever have!'

The hug is fleeting, but it's real. As Hazel lets go and hurries to her little girl, I'm immediately scooped up in another hug, from Dad this time.

'Riley!' he says.

Actually, he *cries*. His shoulders are shaking, his breath coming in gulps.

'Dad, I'm OK, honest!' I assure him, patting his back as if he's the child and I'm the parent.

'Oh, Riley,' he mumbles, his head pressed against mine, 'you are SO like your mother it hurts.'

From the crack in his voice, I know that his heart is breaking.

And, from somewhere deep inside me, I know what I need to do.

Leaving the silky blue bundle nestled in my lap, I lift both my hands and place them gently on his head.

Ha! Who knew the warmth would feel so funny? Prickles and tickles of electricity flow through my fingers, as the gentle heat builds.

Straight away, Dad's shoulders relax, the warmth easing his pain and worry away.

And the angels smile, smile, smile . . . I think they're pretty pleased with their little trainee.

'Riley?' says Dad, beginning to lift his head.

'Yes?' I reply, quickly letting my hands slip away, so this doesn't seem awkward or weird. (Pearl just whispered that instruction to me.)

Dad stares intently at my face, as if he's trying to take every detail of it in or remember it forever. 'I think we need to talk about your mum . . .'

Closer than close . . .

Dad is about to tell me another piece of the puzzle, I'm sure of it.

We're nearly at the top of Folly Hill and I'm so bursting with excitement I feel like yelling, 'JUST TELL ME!' at the top of my voice.

But shy girls like me aren't so good at yelling.

Or should I say, shy girls *who are part angel like me* aren't so good at yelling?

So I do something else.

'Shall we sit over there?' I suggest, pointing to the bench close to the Angel statue.

Sitting on a bench is way too boring for Dot. She

borrowed Bee from the Angelos this morning, so she'll happily scamper off with him and Alastair, playing today's game of let's-be-baby-unicorns. (She's doing a lot of whinnying and trotting.)

Which finally leaves Dad and me alone to talk.

'That was quite some sleep you had last night, Riley,' Dad says with a wry smile, as we park ourselves down on the cold wood of the bench.

'It was, wasn't it?' I laugh, hardly able to believe it was so long, that no one could wake me. Apparently I slept through Dot shaking me, singing me a shouty 'WAKE UP!' song she'd made up and holding a mirror to my face to check that I was still breathing.

My epic sleep was just one reason our promised talk about Mum has had to wait.

Yesterday, Dad and I never had a chance to be on our own anyway. After the lake drama, we all went home in a big family huddle, dropping off Coco on the way.

While Dot was dunked in the bath – to rid her of

chills and muddy lake water – I stood in the shower for forever, washing the grit and grime away, feeling as fresh and new as I'd ever felt.

Then I went to get changed and lay down for a minute – which turned into eighteen hours straight.

'Thank you for tucking me in, by the way,' I tell him. '*And* for the flowers . . .'

I'd fallen asleep on top of my duvet, so Dad had draped the spare one on top of me. I hazily remember feeling the comforting weight of the duvet and the kiss on my forehead. Then he'd propped a sprig of scented lavender beside Mum's photo on my bedside table.

'Not guilty!' says Dad, holding his hands up jokily. 'That was all Hazel's work. She bought the lavender at the Frost Fair, and thought you'd like it in your room.'

'That was nice of her,' I say, blinking with surprise. (It was *Hazel* who'd kissed me goodnight?)

'She's still learning, you know,' Dad says gently. 'How we can all fit together as a family, I mean. She doesn't want to force you into thinking of her as your stepmum, if you're not comfortable with that.'

How funny! All this time, Hazel's been stressing over what I think of her? Sounds like she's been as wary as me. I've always thought she's been a little bit distant, but perhaps she's just been worried that I don't want a replacement mother.

'You know, I think I *could* get used to the idea of her as my stepmum,' I tell Dad, as we watch Dot galumphing around in her wellies.

Things have changed in so many ways after what happened yesterday. Since I plunged into the lake to save her, I've ditched the 'sort of' and even the 'step'. Dot is my sister and I love her. Even if she *does* steal my stuff (I spotted that her toenails were sparkly blue before she put her socks and shoes on to come out).

'Brilliant. That's brilliant, honey,' says Dad, stretching his arm round my shoulders. 'And me loving Hazel doesn't change how much I loved your mum – you know that, don't you?'

'I know,' I say.

We're both quiet and thoughtful for a second, and it's lovely to share a comfortable silence with him. But Dad had better get on with this talk he promised me soon, or I'll be attempting my first-ever spring . . .

'So, about Annie.'

Good. He's not going to let me down (or be a guinea pig for my new powers).

'She was very special, Riley. I mean, *really* special,' Dad begins, rubbing at his face as if he's struggling to know how to say something. 'A total angel.'

'Go on,' I urge him, with the strangest fluttery feeling in my tummy. Does Dad know the truth about her?

'She'd help anyone. Never a thought for herself.'

Oh, OK, he doesn't. To Dad, his lovely wife was just a good kind person – woman, human.

'To be honest, Riley, I wasn't *ever* going to tell you. But I've suddenly realized it's not fair – you need to know what happened the day she . . .'

Dad can't bring himself to say the word 'died', and I can't blame him.

But his distress is like a cold wave sucking him under into a black sea, so I reach for his hand, concentrate hard and hope my first attempt at virtual stroking works.

'She was killed saving a teenage girl, Riley,' Dad carries on, unaware that I know this already, from Friday's spring by the angels. I feel the tension draining from him, muscles relaxing as my own fledgling magic begins to take effect. 'She saw a lorry coming towards the girl, and pushed her out of the way.'

'She was a hero, then?' I say, my heart soaring with pride.

'In some ways, Riley,' Dad replies, lifting his gaze to look straight at me. 'This witness – a man on a motorbike – saw it all. You were in a sling on your mum's chest, but when the lorry hit . . . well, you were somehow flung from the sling. You landed on the road, right by the girl's smashed iPod. But you

only had bruises. Just bruises! Can you believe it? Riley, you could have been as broken as the metal and plastic . . .'

Hold on.

I was in the accident?

I was with Mum till the moment she *died*?

Shock freezes the blood in my veins.

So *this* is why Dad was always so very sad and angry about Mum's death. The fact that Mum left us both behind was awful enough, but he was also torn up inside with anger because she put me in danger that day, that terrible moment. He's missed her *and* blamed her all these years . . .

Suddenly I feel something – the chilly grip of the shock melting with warmth. Somewhere close by, somewhere unseen, the angels are taking care of me.

And now babbles and burblings of whispers fill my head, overlapping so I don't know which angel is saying what.

'*She loved him so much she settled for a human life . . .*'

'*She stepped out into the road, forgetting which world she belonged to . . .*'

'*She thought of herself as pure angel, there to help . . .*'

'*You'll have to take care too, Riley . . .*'

Dad is staring at me, waiting for a reaction, worried what it might be.

'I'm fine, Dad. Mum was a hero,' I say, leaning over to give him a hug.

'Oh, Riley.' Dad sighs with relief at spilling his bottled-up secret at last.

Over his shoulder I can see three dancing dots of light by the stone Angel. I'm glad my friends came; I'm glad they've shared this moment with me. And, after all this time of feeling so far from her, now I know I was close, so close to Mum till the very last second of her life.

'*Told you it would be soon!*' a giggly voice fills my head, and I see one of the dots practically bouncing with delight.

I smile at Pearl, in her non-girl form.

'Stuart, STUART!' Dot suddenly squeals, cantering over to us at high speed, with Alastair bumping behind her, Bee bounding by her side.

'What is it, Dotty?' asks Dad, gently breaking away from our hug.

'I need to get home NOW!' Dot demands. 'It's Coco's princess birthday party soon and I need to get ready and SPARKLY!'

'Do you want to borrow my glittery blue nail varnish again?' I say with a grin, knowing it's hidden in her room somewhere.

'Mmm,' mumbles Dot, biting her lip and wriggling with guilty embarrassment.

I'll let her off this time. I'll give her the big-sister chat later, and tell her she's welcome to borrow my stuff, as long as she asks first – and as long as she promises not to fall in the lake and give me a heart attack ever again.

'Didn't realize that was the time,' Dad says, glancing down at his watch. 'Sorry to cut this short, Riley, but I guess we'd better get going.'

'I think I'll stay for a bit. I'll let Bee run around some more,' I tell him.

'Fair enough,' says Dad, giving me a squeeze of the shoulders before he stands up. 'But we can talk anytime, about anything, OK, Riley? Your mum . . . anything.'

I smile, incredibly happy with that promise. It's all I ever wanted.

Well, that and friendship. When Tia left I had no one, and now there's Sunshine, Kitt and Pearl, Woody and Marnie. Even Etta feels like a friend to me, especially since she knew Mum.

Maybe once Dad and Dot are far enough down the hill, the angels can materialize and we can plan what to do for Etta, figure out how to brighten her world and bring back her –

'Here,' says Dot, turning and running back to me.

She's holding out Alastair. His dopey face is looking straight into mine, his drawn-on tongue lolling. What does she want? For me to give Alastair a kiss bye-bye or something?

'I have a NEW New Year Wish, Riley!' Dot announces. 'It's for Etta to have her OWN doggy. I think it will make her MUCH happier. So can you give her Alastair?'

'What?' I say in surprise. 'But you *love* Alastair.'

'Oh, I don't need him any more now I can have Bee to play with whenever I want!'

And, with a *tra-la-la*, Dot deposits Alastair in my lap and hurries off down the hill after Dad.

With Bee's head resting comfortingly on my lap, I stare after Dad and Dot for the longest time, till the crunchy flint path leads them down into the tangle of streets below.

Then I hear crackling and rustling all around me.

Wings rising, Sunshine and Kitt appear on the bench either side of me.

'Aw, that's so sweet of Dot!' says Pearl, perching on the back of the bench. 'And Etta is going to *adore* him.'

'It's only a stick!' I laugh, gazing around at my three friends.

'Not quite,' says Kitt.

I look down. For the last few minutes I've been lost in my thoughts, absent-mindedly stroking a sea-smoothed, hard hunk of driftwood with doodles drawn on.

But there's been a slight change . . .

'Hey, whoa! Hold on,' I giggle, as the puppy in my lap tries to bounce up and lick my face.

'He's perfect,' says Sunshine. 'He will bring back Etta's shine. Well done, Riley.'

'Well done?' I reply, confused. 'Wasn't it Bee who made this happen?'

But, as I wrestle with the wriggly sausage dog, I feel a tell-tale vibration in my hands. So it *was* me.

Between Dot's kind New Year Wish for Etta and my own brand-new powers, we're going to give Marnie's nan a fresh start.

And the new start starts *now*.

'I'd better take him to her, then,' I say, standing up and aiming for the brow of the hill in the direction of Marnie's house. 'Coming?'

I glance over my shoulder and see the three angels still sitting on the bench, Bee panting happily on the ground. Their eyes shimmer and shine with silver light and love.

'Not this time,' they whisper in quiet words.

That's OK. I can do this on my own. I'm not shy Riley any more; well, not totally.

I give them a wave and go to carry on – then clearly hear Sunshine's voice in my head.

'Hey, do you want to know what the answer is?'

She's sitting tall and serene, red hair dancing in the breeze. Beside her Kitt stares intently at me, and Pearl giggles with delight, obviously knowing what's coming.

'Yes,' I reply in my own quiet words, as the puppy yelps noisily in my arms.

Sunshine's going to tell me what they are, isn't she? What they are, what Mum was, what I'll never be, since I'm rooted here on earth.

'Those random out-of-the-blue moments of sudden joy you can feel. Shafts of sunlight peeking

through the clouds. An answer that comes when your head's been crammed with worries. A daydream. That's us. That's who we are.'

I smile my brightest smile at Sunshine.

I have no idea what she's saying and yet it makes perfect, beautiful sense.

As I walk away I smile up at the stone Angel on her white block and think once again how lucky I am that the angels like me.

Then I laugh to myself when I realize that, after all, now I know the truth, they *are* angels like me.

Angels – just like *me* . . .

Acknowledgements

Big authorly thanks to Wendy, Jennie, Kimberley and Marcus for their sharp eyes and tender tweaks (ooh!).

Make your own friendship bracelet

Friendship bracelets are great fun to make and
even better when you make one with your best
friend! Just follow our step-by-step guide and you'll
have a unique gift – one that's really simple,
but really special to you both!

1. Choose three colours of embroidery thread or old wool – pick any colour
combination you like. Why not check out the 'What colours mean' chart below
and pick colours that represent your friend's character?

2. Take two strands of each colour.

3. Tie a knot at the end of the six strands and separate the different colours
from each other.

4. Get your friend to hold the knotted end of the bracelet and start plaiting the
three colours together – cross the two strands on the left over the two strands
in the middle, and then do the same with the two strands on the right.

5. Repeat this until the bracelet is long enough to go round your wrist,
then tie a knot at the other end.

6. Snip off any straggly ends and tie round your wrist.

7. Now repeat the above to make a second bracelet for your friend!

What colours mean

Red: Enthusiastic   Orange: Friendly   Yellow: Cheerful
Green: Chilled   Blue: Loyal   Purple: Imaginative
Pink: Sweet   Brown: Kind
White: Honest   Black: Deep thinker

www.karenmccombie.com

Create a Friendship Collage

A collage that's all about you and your friends —
that's got to look great on your wall, right? Or why don't
you make one in secret, as a surprise for someone?
Of course, there are websites where you can create an
online collage, but there's nothing like getting a bunch of
photos and images and snipping, sticking and gluing
them together by hand!

1. Decide on the theme.

What do you and your friend(s) like to do together? Share a hobby?
Watch movies? What makes you laugh, squeal, drool? Decide on your theme —
and you're ready for Step 2 . . .

2. Grab some photos.

The snaps you use should be of you as well as your friend(s), or group shots
of you together. Choose a variety of sizes and shapes, as well as photos taken
from different times of your life. (If you don't want to use the ACTUAL photos,
copy them on a printer and use the copies instead.)

3. Flick through some mags or the internet.

Browse through magazines or online to select headlines or images
or even just fun words that represent the theme of your collage.
Rip out the pages or print out your favourites to use. You could also look
for a quote from a film or book that you both love, or maybe even
a phrase you always say to each other.

4. Get creative.

For a cool collage, cut each photo into an interesting shape. If you have a photo of you and a friend, for instance, cut round your bodies and discard the background. Or maybe stick your heads on to a star made out of silver foil, or transplant yourselves on to a funny background, like a scene in Harry Potter!

5. Add the words.

The words and phrases you've picked from magazines or online should be a variety of sizes, shapes, fonts and colours.

6. Get gluing!

Stick the larger images on to a poster board (from art shops) or just some cardboard, and then paste other images around them. Try to cover every area of the backing board with either a photo or words. Remember: you can get clever with your background too – if you don't want to have just one big rectangle, you could cut it into a circle, or even a chunky letter from the alphabet, like the first letter of you or your friend's name.

7. Final touches.

Got any tickets from shows you've been to together? Even tickets from things like swimming or ice skating are nice last-minute additions. And scrabble around for some craft stuff to add sparkle, like bits of ribbon or sequins. Even buttons look cute!

8. Tah-nah!

Your collage is ready. Stick it up on your wall, or present it to your friend. And don't forget – you can always update it by adding a new photo to it now and then.

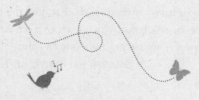

www.karenmccombie.com

How to be an Everyday Angel

The Angelo sisters use their magical abilities to
help Riley – but you don't have to be a real angel
to help others! Check out these six ideas for
how to be an everyday angel . . .

1. Say it, don't think it.

A girl you know has a nice new hairstyle. A boy in class who's usually
annoying has done a great drawing. Your best friend was really good fun today
and made you smile when you were grumpy. You might fleetingly notice and
think about stuff like that, but how about saying something out loud?
Come right out with a compliment? Giving someone a bit of praise can boost
their self-confidence big time. And make you new friends!

2. 'There, there . . .'

Feeling ill is pants. If your friend is off sick with flu or whatever,
be aware that she will be feeling
a) ropey,
b) mopey, and
c) like she's missing out on the fun that you and your other friends are having.
So get yourself round to hers after school or at the weekend, armed with chat,
chocolate and maybe a favourite magazine. Or, if she's infectious,
gather your friends to shout, 'Get well soon!' down the phone to her.
That should help her smile through the snot!

3. Be an ace listener.

You can tell something is bothering your friend, but she keeps saying she's
'fine'. Maybe she doesn't want to talk in front of others, so how about
arranging to have a little time to chat, just the two of you? You can suggest it
face to face, or reach out with a text, or even a note. You might not have all the
answers, but having someone to splurge her feelings to might be
enough to cheer your friend up.

4. 'If you liked that, you might like this...'

Start a book group. And don't just invite your BFs... ask girls you don't know so well, who you know like reading. You might turn people on to books they wouldn't have ever tried before. And, for people who are a little shy, getting together to talk about books and stories and authors is a great way to be sociable. (Don't forget the biscuits — you ALWAYS need biscuits at a book group!)

5. Make homework not suck.

It's easy to get stuck on homework, especially with creative subjects like writing or projects. But being in a group, bouncing ideas around, can really flick a switch on in your brain!

So suggest get-togethers to help each other out — but lay down the rules too:

1) be nice (no poo-pooing what people say),

2) be encouraging (you'd want the same) and

c) no gossiping (you can save that for later, once the homework is done!).

6. Mad makeover time!

If a friend is feeling a little flat or fed-up, get silly with an over-the-top makeover. Invite her round, blast some music on, and try out a ton of different hairstyles and make-up looks on her. Get her to pose in the mirror, or catwalk up and down the bedroom. It'll be even more fun if you get her to do the same to you!

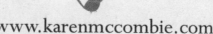
www.karenmccombie.com

 # Listen

Do you love listening to stories?

Want to know what happens behind the scenes in a recording studio?

Hear funny sound effects, exclusive author interviews and the best books read by famous authors and actors on the **Puffin Podcast** at www.puffinbooks.com

#ListenWithPuffin